Th

Convenient Bride

A BWWM Billionaire Romance By..

CJ HOWARD

Summary

Billionaire Peter has found that his reputation for being a playboy is beginning to have a very negative effect on his business. So he needs a wife to help him shed his playboy image and he is willing to do what it takes to make it happen.

Emmaline is a woman with a heart of gold with big plans for her life but her job as a waitress does not make it easy for her to get where she wants to be. A payment of $3 million dollars to be the convenient bride of a billionaire for 3 years would set her up for life and it is not one she is going to turn down.

This was meant to be just a simple marriage of convenience with a clear end date and with both getting exactly what they want. However, once Peter takes time to get know Emmaline he begins to wonder if he ever wants this to end....

Copyright Notice

Contents

Chapter1

It was a warm spring evening down in the French Quarter of New Orleans, and a full scale party was hopping at the Ritz Carlton Hotel on Canal Street. A fund raiser was being held for the Governor to get him reelected, and all of the swankiest people were there. Politicians and businessmen were surrounded by beautiful women and everyone was smiling, dancing, and drinking, which is the rule of the day in the Quarter.

His limousine pulled up to the front door of the building, and Peter stepped out of the car, ran his hand through his tousled golden hair, flashed a brilliant smile at some of the women standing at the entrance to the hotel, and winked his emerald green eyes at them. They giggled and waved, grinning back at him like all women did. He strode into the hotel and glanced at himself in a mirror he passed. He looked good, and he knew it. He was wearing a dark green silk shirt and white pants that clung to his body in just the right places and left a little mystery in others. He dressed with style every day, with the intent of drawing women in and maintaining his very fashionable and classy appearance.

Peter didn't get fifteen feet into the ballroom before men were glad-handing him and women were hugging him and kissing his cheek. They lingered around him, holding his hands, rubbing his back, and touching his face. Women had been this way with him since his voice had deepened and he vanquished puberty. He smiled and his dimples drew sighs and grins from the ladies who were gazing at him. There was a deep one in each cheek, a slight cleft in his chin, and a chiseled jaw that was usually sporting a three day beard.

He had a drink in his hand almost immediately and he took a long pull on it as two local politicians tried to bend his ear about contributions to their causes, while one of the women who had sidled up close to him when he walked in slid her arm around his waist and subtly dropped her hand to give his backside a firm squeeze. He didn't flinch or even blink as the two men before him blathered on about their topics, he just reached his own hand down passed the woman's hip and squeezed her back. She grinned and pressed her body up against the side of his, watching him as though he was the only man in the room.

Peter nodded at the men and asked them to email his assistant Nelson, and then he walked away from them and the woman walked with him. She pulled him to the side of the crowd of people and ran her hands up his chest, then held his face and kissed him hotly. He welcomed the distraction, and he kissed her back and rubbed his hands firmly over her hips. Then he let her go and tapped his finger on her nose and told her she was as sweet as a magnolia, and then he walked away from her, even though she tried to follow him and call after him.

He waded through the throng of people and finished three drinks before he made it all the way through the party in the ballroom. By that point, he was already fed up with them. He stopped at a bar in the emptiest corner of the room and refilled his glass of champagne. As he was standing there, he heard a soft voice and he looked up to see a gorgeous woman in a skintight red satin dress and high heels. Her curled blonde hair hung over her shoulders and formed crescents around her voluptuous breasts. Her full red lips curved into a smile and she gazed at him from aqua blue eyes. Peter let his appreciative gaze wander slowly over her body and then he smiled back at her. She had to be in her early twenties. She could have been a centerfold model, and might have been, for all he knew. Knowing women as well as he did, he would peg her at twenty-five.

"You look like I imagined you right into existence," he said in a low, smooth voice.

She took a step closer to him and tilted her head. "You look like you've had your fill of this place and this truly maddening crowd."

He knew right where she was going. He smiled and tilted his champagne glass back until it was empty. "I was done with it before I got here, at least until now. You're the only thing that might keep me here just a little bit longer."

She leaned forward and took his glass from his hand and set it on the bar. "Oh, I don't think either one of us needs to be here any longer. Would you like to take a walk with me?" She slid her hand into his elbow and looked up at him expectantly.

"I was hoping you would save me from all this." He smiled at her and she grinned back, and then they slipped out of a side door and down the hall away from the event.

"Where are we off to?" he asked conspiratorially.

"Oh, I thought I would show you around the hotel, starting with the elevator and ending in the suite I am staying in. How does that sound?" she asked as she pulled him into the elevator with her and wrapped her arms around his neck. He grinned and pulled her close to him.

"It sounds inviting, and very..." he leaned down and brushed his lips lightly over hers, just enough to tease her, "…enticing." He smiled as she opened her mouth and trailed her tongue over his lips.

Her hand slid down to his groin and she began to caress him as he grew thick and solid beneath her fingers. She lifted her other hand to his face and gently pressed the fiery red tip of her fingernail into the dimple on one of his cheeks. "You are so beautiful." she said, looking into his mesmerizing green eyes, and then she opened her mouth to taste his. He raised his hands to her breasts, cupping them and rubbing his fingers over her hardening nipples as they strained against the thin red material, reaching out for his touch.

The elevator bell rang and the doors slid open. She walked him to the suite she was staying in and closed the door behind him as he walked into it. He stood in a well-appointed living room and looked at her as she sauntered toward him, swaying like a cat ready to pounce on its prey.

"You know, you look familiar to me. What's your name?" he asked, wondering where he had seen her face before.

"Carolyn," she replied, as she took him by the hand and led him to the bedroom. She stopped him at the side of the bed and slipped his trousers off of him, delighted to find that he wasn't wearing anything underneath his pants. She stripped his shirt from him and ran her hands over his sculpted body, trailing her tongue over his smooth skin as she lowered herself to her knees before him. He groaned deeply as his desire grew and her mouth devoured him, somehow taking the fullness of him over her tongue and into her throat. He slid his hands into her thick blonde waves of hair and his fingers curled snugly around the back of her head as she drew his heat and pleasure almost to the tip of him, but he stopped her and said in a low voice, "Not yet, baby, I want much more of you than that."

Carolyn released him and stood up before him. He grasped her hungrily, turning her so that her back was to his chest and he held her tightly to him, moving one hand to cup her breast, pinching her rock hard nipple between his thumb and forefinger as his other hand slid up her leg under her dress. His fingers found her panties and moved beneath them, massaging her core and then dipping into her and moving swiftly over her.

She gasped and cried out in pleasure as he touched his lips to her ear and whispered, "Come for me, Carolyn…" and she did. It excited him enormously.

"Come again..." he told her, his fingers moving even more deftly within her, and moments later she reached her arms back and clutched at the back of his head, crying out as she quivered in his grasp and her orgasm overwhelmed her.

Peter pulled her onto the bed with him and settled her so that she was straddling him. He ran his hands up her thighs, shoving the thin red material up as he went. He leaned in close to her and moved his lips over her skin, tasting her and biting at her gently until he reached her tiny panties. One quick snap of his practiced hands, and they were ripped off of her without a mark. She laughed for a moment, but her excitement became a loud gasp as he buried his tongue in her body and clenched his hands to the back of her, holding her tightly to his ravenous mouth as he moved his tongue nimbly over and into her, bringing her to orgasm in mere moments. When he had tasted her pleasure, he peeled her dress off of her and tossed it onto the floor, and then lowered her onto his anxiously awaiting erection.

His hands canvassed her full round breasts, squeezing them and pulling them to him as his mouth closed over her hard pink nipples and he thrust himself deeply into her. Peter's hands moved over her body from her breasts to her hips, clenching her and holding her tightly to him as he filled her depths with his thick heat, moving lustfully while trying to hold back his own orgasm and take his time savoring every moment with her.

Carolyn rode his body with an erotic rhythm that sent thrills all over him, and he moved his mouth from her hard and twisting tongue to the buds of her nipples and then back to her hungry red lips again.

She grew more excited as he made her come again and again, and being bound up in her excitement, he could not hold his own ecstasy back any longer; he flooded her with his own heated pleasure, making her cry out in exhaustion and bliss.

She collapsed on his chest and giggled with a tired sigh, then looked up at him and kissed him softly. "You are so delicious," she whispered. "I wish I could keep you for a while."

He pushed her hair out of her face and kissed her back. "No one keeps me," he said with a sympathetic tone.

"Well, I'm going to keep you here with me just a little longer before I let you go." She grinned at him. She rose up off of him and began massaging his body. His muscles melted at her touch and in no time, he was relaxed and felt like he could have a really good nap, until her tongue and mouth began to slide over his groin again and he stiffened with need once more. She pulled him to kneeling position and then she bent over in front of him, facing the foot of the bed. He smiled down at her and slowly pushed himself into the warm, wet depths of her, inch by inch, until he was fully inside, and then with his hands clamped on her hips, he began to pump himself into her again, and they both moaned and cried out loud in pleasure until the doors of the room opened and they were frozen in shock at the sight of an old man in his seventies, wearing a dark blue suit and a red tie, standing in front of them. He was flanked by photographers, reporters and new crews.

Peter blinked in surprise. “Governor Collins!” he breathed out.

The Governor glared down at the woman Peter’s body was buried in. “Carolyn!” he shouted.

She gasped and in the moment that her mouth fell open in horror, the cameras clicked and flashed brightly for what seemed like an eternity before the Governor stepped into the room and closed the doors behind him.

Peter pulled himself from Carolyn’s body and covered himself with a sheet as she bounced out of the bed and grabbed a robe from a nearby chair. The Governor looked at them both furiously.

“What in the hell are you doing?” he demanded.

She ran up to him and grasped his arm, but he shook her hands away. Peter was dressed in record time and turned to look at the old man again. “Governor, I guess you must know Carolyn?” he asked without blushing.

“She’s my wife!” he shouted at Peter.

Peter nodded and pursed his lips. "I am sorry about that, Sir. I didn't know who she was. I'll be going."

The Governor tried to launch himself at Peter, but Carolyn grabbed him and pulled him away as Peter slipped through the bedroom doors and into the living room of the suite, where the Governor's aides were sitting. One of the men turned and looked at him with thinly veiled rage.

"We are trying to get him re-elected, you moron!" the young man railed at him. Peter lifted his hands in the air in silent apology, and then quickly let himself out of the room only to be greeted by a throng of reporters and cameras just waiting for him to emerge.

The elevator took its time getting to him and though he turned his back to the news crews, they hassled him until the doors of the elevator closed and gave him some privacy.

Peter sighed and silently berated himself for not checking to find out who the woman was. Typically, he wasn't concerned with whether or not the women he slept with were married or seeing someone else. In his opinion, that just wasn't his business. It was up to the woman if she wanted to have an affair. He was only interested in the time they shared intimately, and when that was over, he was gone, so it didn't matter to him what they did before or after his encounters with them. This one, however, was slightly different. He'd been invited to the Governor's fundraiser so that he would contribute money to the re-election campaign for the man, not to mattress wrestle his wife in their suite during the event.

The fact that the reporters literally caught them in the act made it that much worse. Peter was a local prominent businessman, and he knew it would be a black eye from which he might never recover. He texted his driver and had his car waiting for him as he slipped out of a side door from the hotel as quickly and quietly as he could, wishing he could leave it all behind him.

*

Two weeks later, the papers were still buzzing about his illicit affair, and photos of him buried hip deep in Carolyn were splashed all over the pages of the newspapers, magazines, and all over the internet. He was advised by his assistant, Nelson, that he should stay out of the public as much as possible and focus on his business deals. It was crucial that he made no further mistakes of any sort, so he stayed in the office of his mansion and worked from there.

He'd been making plans to refurbish some of the area in and around the French Quarter that had been severely damaged by the last major hurricane. Prior to his flagrant affair, he had just scheduled a meeting with some of the city's officials and business owners to collaborate with him on the project. He poured all of his efforts into preparing an airtight presentation; one that would convince all of them to cut through the notorious red tape that the city officials wrapped the city in and work with him to make the refurbishment a major success. New Orleans needed the facelift, and he knew he was the right man to do it. He just needed to convince everyone else of it.

The day of the meeting finally came, and he rode in the limo to a charming little restaurant down in the Quarter, near the area he wanted to work on. He had secured a private room for the evening and arranged for a Creole dinner to be served to all of them. When he entered the meeting, it was obvious that his reputation had preceded him. The men and women who attended were cold and quiet towards him, and there were several people who had said they would attend and then bowed out after his tumble with the Governor's wife.

He stood tall and acted every bit the gracious and humble host of the evening, seeing to any of the slightest needs of his guests, and having dinner and cocktails served to them while he made his presentation. He just hoped it was enough.

Peter hit the nail on the head. He could not have delivered his proposal any better. The men and women who were present had begun the evening with cold disregard for him, and though he had plied them with wine and whiskey throughout the evening, as well as some of the best food to be cooked up in the Quarter, they still saw the benefit to the community in the endeavors he was suggesting that they undertake.

At the end of the evening, he could not tell if they were fully sold or not, and he felt his stomach drop when one of the more prominent business owners of the neighborhood spoke up after he ended his presentation.

"Peter, there is no doubt that what you have shown us tonight would be a tremendous help to the community, but I'm going to be honest with you. Not a single person in this room is interested in doing any sort of business with you right now. Your deplorable behavior has disgraced this town with a shame that it rarely sees, and that's saying something for a place that boasts the tawdriest of celebrations in the country. I'd like to be a part of something like this, but not with you at the helm of it. Thank you for your time and your ideas, Peter." Then the man rose up and walked out of the room without even shaking Peter's hand. The others agreed, though more subtly, and all of them followed suit.

He watched them go and sank into a chair at one of the tables. The waitress came to him and handed him a tumbler of whiskey.

“Here. This one is on me,” she said, knowing that he needed it pretty badly.

“Thanks,” he mumbled. He took a swig of it and raked his fingers through his golden hair. “I can’t believe it went that badly.” He let out a sigh.

She’d watched the whole meeting and she knew his intentions were good, but she also realized that no one was going to let him do anything because of his recent scandal, among many other indiscretions. She looked at him sitting there in misery and decided to talk with him about it. “They are right. You have good ideas. They need some work, but you have really good ideas, and what you want to do would benefit the community, but no one wants to rebuild anything with a playboy who doesn’t have a care in the world.”

He looked up at her sharply and paused for a moment. He hadn’t bothered to look at her at any point that night and she had been their private server through the entire meeting. She stood before him, her hand on the curve of her hip, her head tilted and her hair pulled up in braids around her head. She had a dark caramel color to her skin and warm dark brown eyes. Her body was curvy and petite, her limbs muscular, and her facial features delicate and soft. He blinked up at her as she looked down at him. He struggled to remember what it was she had said, and then her words cut into him again and he drew in his breath to respond.

"I do have a care! I care quite a bit!" He felt annoyed about her calling him a playboy, but he couldn't deny it at all.

"I know that. I watched your presentation. I can see that you care. The people in here can see that you care, but no one outside of this room has any idea at all that you care about anything but women, drinking and parties. You have one of the worst reputations in the state," she said, not feeling the slighted bit of guilt. She knew he had to hear it, and she was fairly certain that no one else would ever tell him. She began clearing away dishes and bottles and his eyes followed her as he spoke back to her.

"I didn't know that was the Governor's wife! I thought she was just some woman at the party. Just another woman coming on to me who wanted to have a good time!" He raised his voice defensively, but hoped not to attract any attention.

She felt miffed at his attitude and wasn't shy about telling him why. "You are out with different women all the time. You think the people who live here don't see you? You think they don't know that? Your reputation didn't come from that one incident. No, no. You have a terrible reputation from one side of Louisiana to the other, and it's been building for years. It isn't that you don't have good ideas, and it isn't that people don't want to make changes around here for the better, but no one wants your hand in anything they do because your hands are dirty, and no one wants to touch what's dirty," she said with finality as she walked out of the room with a loaded tray and he watched the door close behind her. Minutes later she came back with a fresh glass of whiskey for him, and as she set it down, he looked up at her and spoke with a softer tone.

"Sit down with me for a minute, will you?" he asked miserably.

She had a few minutes and he looked like he didn't have a friend in the world. She felt sorry for him in a way, but there was also a part of her that didn't trust him fully. She lowered her brows at him and frowned but he picked up the glass of booze with both hands and tilted his head at her. "I will wrap my dirty hands around this glass and I promise not to touch you with them. I just want to talk a bit more. No one ever talks to me with the honesty that you are giving me."

She looked at him suspiciously, but she sat down near him all the same and looked at him.

"You seem to know a lot about my reputation. How is that?" he asked, not looking forward to the answer.

"People talk. You're a rich guy around town. Everyone knows what you're doing. Sometimes it's in the papers, but most of the time it's just because you are one of the things that people talk about around here. The talk isn't good. It's never good when it's about you. People don't like the way you act and the way you live, and part of it isn't their business, but the other part is that you have a public image, and it's pretty badly tarnished," she said with thoughtful honesty, looking at him closely. He really was as gorgeous as everyone had said, and the photos she had seen of him did him no justice at all, but she saw the rest of him; the bad, right along with his beautiful exterior, and it was like looking at two sides of a coin at the same time.

He rubbed his fingers over his forehead. "I didn't know it was that bad," he said in a quiet tone.

"It is that bad, and nothing is going to change that until you change your image," she told him. "No one is going to want to do anything with you. You would get a lot further with the people of this city if you had a better reputation. You need to think about changing that before you try to start changing neighborhoods around here, because all you're going to do is spin your wheels in the mud if you try to do it the way things are now." She knew that the truth she was telling him was hurting him, but she knew he probably needed to hear it, and she felt like telling him might help drive him to change.

He furrowed his brow, looking at her more closely, "What's your name?"

"Emmaline," she said, holding her hand out to him.

He looked at her hand and took it in his slowly, shaking it and looking up at her, "You aren't opposed to touching a man with dirty hands?" he asked.

She shrugged her shoulders. "Everyone gets their hands dirty, but not everyone is as well-known as you are. You aren't the first man to sleep with a married woman. It's just that your indiscretion was published for the whole world to see, so everyone feels like they can look down on you and forget their own sins. People wouldn't be so hard on you if everyone had all their bad deeds made public." She knew that sentiment was true, at the very least.

He listened quietly to her, his gaze steady on her face, "Emmaline. That's a pretty name. Where did you get it?"

"I was named after my grandmother. She passed on, though, so now it's just me and my grandfather, Henri." She was proud of her grandparents. They had raised her and they were the best people she knew. She was honored to be named after her grandmother. Emmaline withdrew her hand from his and moved to stand up, but he stopped her.

"Wait! Please don't go yet. You've really given me a lot to think about and I feel like you have a bit more insight that I ought to look into before you leave. Please," he asked earnestly, and she pressed her lips together for a moment in consideration and then sat back down.

"Alright. What else do you want to talk about?" she asked, looking back at him.

"Well, you've told me how bad things are, and that I will have to change all of it before I can try to work with the people around here to change the neighborhood, but… how do I change my image? If it's so bad, how do I dig myself out of that hole?" He lifted his whiskey and took a long drink.

She leaned back in her chair and looked at him. "You're serious? You really want to know?" She wasn't sure he did want to know what she had to say to him.

He closed his eyes and nodded. “I really want to know.”

Emmaline thought to herself that he had asked for it. She planted her hands on her knees and shook her head. “Your image is one of a wild playboy. If you want the people around here to trust you and look up to you, you need to develop a new image. You should try to be a family man. At least get a wife, even if you aren’t interested in having children. Have a steady relationship with a respectable, well brought up woman who truly cares about the people here and the community, someone who is honest and kind, thoughtful, helpful, generous, and has the best interests of the city at heart, and get serious with her and then marry her. Change your image enough that people see the two of you as a couple; a unit that works together instead of just you as a single playboy. Act as one solitary unit that wants to make a difference here and people will see you that way and they will want to work with you and make changes for the better. That’s the way you ought to do it. Nothing else is going to make them forget all of those pictures they've seen in the paper and online." She watched him to see what he would think of that, and he looked like he was going to be sick.

Her words struck deeply at him. A wife. A serious relationship. He had bucked against just that ideal all of his life, and for no specific reason other than that he was adamantly against himself settling down with one woman. The idea was completely alien to him. He couldn't conceive of it at all.

Peter shook his head. "There has to be another way. What else could I do?" he pleaded.

She shook her head back at him, her sympathy waning. "That's it, there is no other way. People won't stop looking at you like you're a playboy unless you show them that you aren't a playboy anymore, and the only way to do that is to change it for real. You're going to have to grow up and get serious with some woman, a respectable woman, before anyone starts to take you seriously." She could tell by the expression on his face that nothing she said was going to convince him of that, and she felt like anything else she might tell him would be wasted.

He was thoroughly repulsed by the idea and he lifted his whiskey to his lips with a scowl on his face. She just looked away from him and shrugged again. "Well, that's the only way you're going to change it." She stood up and walked toward the door.

"Thank you, Emmaline. I appreciate the time you gave me and your insight. You gave me a lot to think about," he said as she turned and waved at him before she disappeared.

***

When he got up the next day, the idea that Emmaline had discussed with him the night before was still on his mind. No longer rattling around, it fell like a seed onto good soil and it had begun to sprout tender little roots and grow.

Peter called his assistant to meet him in his office at home. Nelson arrived early and sat across from Peter at his desk.

"How did the meeting go last night, sir?" Nelson asked with interest.

"The message was well received, but the messenger was not. It seems that my mistakes have jaded the opinions of those around me, enough so that none of them are interested in associating with me and doing business with me, even at the cost of improving and refurbishing devastated areas of the city." Peter had come to terms with it before he had even gotten home the night before.

Nelson frowned and shifted uncomfortably in his seat. "Well, that's truly unfortunate, sir," he replied with disappointment.

Peter looked at him and interlocked his fingers, resting his hands on his desk. "Nelson, are you aware that my reputation is basically shot in the entire state of Louisiana? Have you heard that?" he asked, hoping for the best possible answer.

Nelson looked down and pursed his lips and then looked back up at his boss, "Yes, Sir, I am aware of that, and I have heard it quite a few times."

Peter scowled at him and looked away, "Well, then why haven't you ever said anything to me about it before?"

"Well, sir, you never asked about it, so I thought you knew. I supposed that you were aware of it.

Certainly you must be, when no one has anything good to say about you." Nelson began to look confident about what he was saying to his employer, as though he was telling him something that was helpful without being hurtful. Or like he had been holding it in for quite some time.

Peter closed his eyes for a moment and soaked in the words he heard, and then he looked at Nelson and put his hands on the desk. "What methods would you say are my best options for improving my public image, Nelson?"

"I'd say good works, even the project that you are working on to improve and refurbish the areas that need help in the city. Also, it wouldn't hurt if you stopped making your love life public." Nelson blushed slightly at the mention of Peter's love life.

Peter gazed at him, green eyes blazing, "What if no one will work with me to help me accomplish the good works you're talking about?"

Nelson opened his mouth but then closed it again right away. He didn't have a ready answer for that. "Well, sir, I guess you'll just have to do as many on your own as you can until people decide that they want to start working with you again."

"There was a young lady last night who had another idea. I thought I'd run it past you," Peter said with a determined tone.

Nelson was all ears. "Oh, of course, sir. Please. What did she have to say?"

"It's good that you're sitting down," Peter smirked sarcastically to himself. "She said she thinks I ought to have a serious monogamous relationship with a respectable woman and then marry her so that my image would be that of a devoted husband and family man. What do you think of that?"

Nelson couldn't help himself, and his initial reaction was to snort, because he had tried to hold in his shock and laughter and he couldn't keep it in. The snort erupted in a full loud laugh at the completely ridiculous notion of Peter being with only one woman and then marrying her. It was beyond the scope of his reality.

"Has she met you?" Nelson asked satirically. Then he realized that Peter was still being serious and he straightened his tie and his posture and looked back at his boss with a stoic expression. “I’m sorry, sir. My thoughts are that for anyone else, that might be a very good idea, but monogamous relationships and marriage aren’t exactly your… cup of tea, sir.”

Peter sighed. “I realize that, Nelson. Your mirth is inappropriate. I’m trying to accomplish a rejuvenation in the city and I need help, not sarcasm.” He leaned back in his chair and rubbed his chin thoughtfully. “Do you think there’s any other way for me to fix my image in a short period of time?”

Nelson considered it thoughtfully and shook his head, “No, sir. I think she was right on about what you said, a serious relationship and marriage is about the best way to fix it. It would show everyone that you’ve settled down and taken some responsibility for your life and that would attract members of the community who tend to live more ethical and moral lives. She’s right on about it, come to think of it.”

Peter bit his lip. “How do you suppose I tackle that monster?” he asked, hoping for a miracle.

Nelson stood up and walked around the room, hands in his pants pockets, thinking deeply on it for a few minutes. After pacing back and forth for a short while, he came back to his chair and sat at the edge of it, looking at Peter with some hope.

"I have an idea. It's an immoral idea, and unethical, but it might work," he said with a smile.

"Isn't that kind of defeating the purpose?" Peter frowned.

"No… not really. Actually, I think it would be your saving grace," he answered thoughtfully. "Here's the plan. We find a woman for you who is morally upstanding, honest, considerate, smart, beautiful, hardworking; someone that the public can fall in love with, and we have you date her for a little while, get you both right in the middle of the public eye, and then you marry her, but it's under contract. Let's say, just for discussions, a three year contract, and during that time you do all the public works you want to do, accomplish what you want to achieve, and then the contract ends and the two of you get an amicable divorce. You both part as close friends. You pay her a set sum of money, something considerable, and she keeps the secret. You rent a wife. She makes money, you get your projects completed and you improve your public image. If you feel like you need to see other women, it won't hurt your marriage because she is basically an employee of yours, because you rented her, and there is no emotional tie there. If you do see other women, you go out of state to do it. No one finds out, and voila, you have the best of both worlds." Nelson let out a breath and beamed, quite proud of himself for coming up with such a brilliant plan.

Peter stared at him. "You must be kidding, Nelson. Rent a wife?" He stood up out of his chair and leaned over the desk, glaring at his assistant. "*Rent a wife?* For three years? Who's going to do that? Who is going to put up with me as my rental wife for three whole years?" He paced around the desk and flung his hands up in the air. "Where are we going to find a woman who won't mind being around me that long, who knows how I am and is interested in helping to make me look like a better man, who is willing to take money for a crazy idea like this, who is upstanding and respectable, who is honest and trustworthy… who is beautiful and who the city could fall… in… love… with.” He stopped and his eyes grew wide. “I know who. *I know who!*” He dashed out the door and drove himself downtown.

Emmaline was cleaning off a table when he walked in the door of the restaurant and his eyes looked around and stopped when they reached her. She took a deep breath and stood up, her cleaning rag in her hand and a pretty good idea in her head that whatever he was coming in to her restaurant for, it couldn’t be good.

He stopped in front of her. “I need to talk with you,” he said simply.

She lowered her brow. She didn’t like his tone. “I’m working.”

Peter looked around at the restaurant; it was dead. “It’s slow. This will only take a little while. Can you take a break? We’ll go somewhere for coffee. Low key, my treat.”

Emmaline scowled at him. "What do you think you're playing at? I'm not the kind of girl that goes around-"

He cut her off, "I know! I know you're not like that. That's why I want to talk with you. Come on, Emmaline, this is all your idea anyway, you started it. I've come up with a plan to fix my reputation and I need your help. Please. Just give me fifteen minutes, okay?" He pleaded with her and she glared at him. "Please?" he asked again and she rolled her eyes and handed him the cleaning rag.

"Here. Wash this table. I'll go talk to my manager." She grabbed his hand and dropped the rag into it and he looked down at it and stared at it, then looked back up at her with a clueless expression on his face as she walked away.

Emmaline talked very quietly to another woman at the counter, pointing subtly at Peter, and then she rolled her eyes and shrugged her shoulder. He turned and began wiping the cloth over the table, peeking over his shoulder at her. It was a moment before he realized he had never cleaned a table in his life. He stared down at the rag and the table and blinked in wonder.

She came back to him and put her hands on her hips. "Alright, we can go for a quick coffee." Then she leaned over and yanked the cleaning rag from his hand and frowned at the table. "What do you think you're doing? That's no way to wipe a table down! You're fired. Let's go." She tossed the rag in a bucket and waved at the lady behind the counter who watched them leave with raised eyebrows and no small amount of opinionated judgment on her face.

They walked to a café a few blocks away and sat together at a table in the corner. Emmaline had her back to the room in hopes that no one would recognize her with the scourge of the city. He noticed her behavior and looked at her questioningly.

"Let me get this right, *you* don't want to be seen with *me*?" he asked in amazement.

She tilted her head slightly at him and raised her eyebrows. "Did you really just ask me that? Would *you* want to be seen with you? People like me around here. I have a good reputation, and I'd like to keep it *thank you very much*."

He slouched a bit and felt his courage begin to waver. "Well, that's not going to help me all that much if you don't want to be seen with me."

She lowered one eyebrow at him in consternation. "What are you talking about?" she asked carefully.

Peter reached both his hands across the table and touched her hand, but she jerked her hand away from him and gave him a warning glare. He sighed and put his hands in his lap. "Sorry! I just… I just need to talk with you about this, uh… idea that came up between my assistant and me. It stemmed from something you said, and so I thought I'd… come talk to you about it."

"Well? What is it?" she asked, with suspicion.

Peter raked his fingers through his golden hair and took a deep breath. "It's ah… it's kind of complicated. It's still sort of a raw idea, still in the making, but I think that it will… uh… it will work out pretty well." He looked back at her nervously. "Maybe."

She leaned toward him and said in a sharp undertone, “You have fifteen more minutes. You better use it wisely and get to the point already.”

He leaned forward and lowered his voice even further. “Well, you said I should find a girl and be monogamous with her, and then get married. I um… I found the girl. It’s you,” he said and before he could take a breath and continue, she jumped straight up from her chair and snapped at him.

“*What?* Have you lost your *damn mind?!*”

He reached for her arms to pull her back down to her seat, but she yanked herself away from him before he could reach her. “Wait! Wait! It’s not what you think! It’s a business arrangement! It’s not a real marriage!”

She stared at him and her mouth fell open slightly. “You have lost your mind. It just went an wandered off, probably up some girl’s skirt.”

He looked around at the other patrons in the café who were beginning to give them curious looks. He smiled at them as if it was nothing, and then he motioned toward her chair. “Would you please sit down? You're causing a scene. Listen, it's not at all what you think. Just hear me out. Please!" He resorted to pleading with her again and she sighed and sat back down in the chair.

"Fine. Finish your piece," she said with a rebellious glare on her face.

Peter leaned toward her and lowered his voice substantially. "I was listening last night when you told me that I need to get my public image straightened out. I was listening to you when you told me that I need to have a good woman in my life. A respectable, well brought up woman who truly cares about the people and the community, someone honest and kind, thoughtful, helpful, generous, and someone who has the best interests of the city at heart. That's pretty much exactly what you told me last night. I got to thinking about it, and I talked to my assistant, and he agreed with you and then he came up with this idea. I need a wife, but obviously I don't have a lot of time and I don't really want to get involved with anyone on a serious level. I like my freedom. I like not having a monogamous relationship and I don't want to commit myself to anyone for the rest of my life, so here's the best possible solution to this tangle of challenges. I rent you as my wife for three years and-"

"You *what?!*" she seethed at him and narrowed her eyes, leaning toward him slightly and whispered through her teeth. "You want to *rent me*? What kind of woman do you think I am?!" The volume of her voice began to increase marginally. "I am not the kind of girl who sells herself to-"

He cut her off again, "No! Wait! I'm not trying to buy you, I just want to rent you for three-" She picked up her cup of water and tossed it right in his face. He sputtered for a moment and looked like he was in complete shock.

Emmaline stood up and turned to leave, but he grabbed her arm and held her back. She turned and glared at him furiously. "You take your hands off of me!" she spat at him.

He looked at her unapologetically, "I still have about twelve minutes, and you haven't let me explain the whole thing to you. Please, Emmaline, just sit down and hear me out. No fighting, no yelling, and no more water. Just listen to me. You're just about my only hope of making that project happen to repair and refurbish the neighborhood."

She scowled at him and he let go of her arm and pulled her chair out for her. "Please?" he asked quietly. She sat and folded her hands in her lap and then looked at him with narrow eyes.

"Alright. I'm sitting. I'll listen to the whole thing. You have twelve minutes. Go," she said in a quiet warning voice.

He sat and began speaking in a soft voice. "So Nelson was saying to me that he thinks-"

"Who is Nelson?" she interrupted.

"He's my assistant," Peter answered, glad that she had an actual question rather than another fit. "He said he thinks the best thing for me, since I don't want a real committed relationship, is to find a woman who fits our description, or rather, your description, and get her to let me hire her on as a pseudo wife, a pretend wife, for three years. I would rent her. I'd pay her for her time and work as a public wife, not a private wife, because I don't want that, and she could help me clean up my image and do what you said… about working as a unit to help the community, and then after three years she could be free to go. We get an amicable divorce, she is paid the whole time, and I'd even make a lump sum at the end for her, and the whole time we live as business partners, but she shows the public that we are married and it makes me look like a respectable businessman rather than a trashy playboy. Remember all your ideas? Well, this is what they've come to. That whole thing was your idea, except for the part about renting the wife, but really, let's be honest, that's the best possible scenario for me and any poor woman who decides I'm a case worth helping and actually takes up with me for three whole years."

Emmaline watched him carefully and listened as he continued.

"I just thought I would ask you, because you seem to really fit the bill kind of perfectly. You love the community, you're a woman of high morals and values, and as you said, you have a good reputation.

This would be a way for you to help me get that project done. You said yourself that all my ideas were good."

"I said they were good, but they needed some work," she intoned quietly, watching him closely.

"You're waitressing right now, which means you probably aren't making much money. This project means a great deal to me. I really want to see it happen. We might be coming from two very different places, but we both want the same things for the city, and together, we could make that happen. It will just take a little sacrifice from both of us-"

"A little?!" she scowled at him.

"Some sacrifice from me and a lot from you, and together we could do this and make it happen. Think of it as a job. You'd have your own room at my house, you'd be paid a tidy sum and have your own car and you could spend your time helping out those who really need it instead of wiping down tables at the restaurant. Surely you could use some extra money." He was out of good reasons for her to help him. All but one. "Besides, I don't really have many friends, at least none that are real, true friends, and people who are honest with me to my face. You are definitely the most honest and upfront person I know. If you need some time to think about it, go ahead, but this is something I want to start as soon as possible so I can get that project going." He sat back in his chair and sighed, sipping his coffee, thinking how thankful he was that she hadn't tossed that at him.

She tilted her head and considered him. He was being truthful and he was being genuine, and those were two things she valued highly. She'd have her own room, and he didn't want a relationship, so that took a huge worry out of her mind, but not fully from her thoughts.

"What about sex?" she asked, and he choked on his coffee.

"*What?*" he gasped, looking at her with wide eyes.

"Are you going to expect sex from this pretend wife of yours?" she asked again, looking at him with suspicion.

He shook his head adamantly. "No. Not at all. This is strictly business, one hundred percent down the line. No sex. No fooling around, no physical contact except things like holding hands in public, and maybe an occasional kiss on the cheek for the cameras when the press is around. Just enough to be convincing. That's it." He looked at her and she raised one eyebrow in uncertainty.

"Honestly! I'm not going to start anything with any woman living under my roof. Not that I ever thought there would be a woman living under my roof," he grumbled slightly.

Her expression softened, though she regarded him carefully still. "How tidy a sum of money are we talking about?"

"How much would you want?" he asked. "It seems fair to me that a million and a half ought to be enough. That comes out to five hundred thousand a year. That should be alright, don't you think?"

She gaped at him in disbelief. "*What!*"

He lowered his head and looked at the floor. "Oh, alright. Three million. You'd be doing a lot of public events. Plus… you are putting up with me."

He raised his head and looked at her. She was staring at him with wide eyes.

"If you do it," he said, and sipped his coffee.

She continued to stare at him, seemingly adding up figures in her head.

He sipped his coffee again.

"So… will you do it?" he asked, feeling uncomfortable under the lock of her stare.

She shook her head. "I can't believe I'm going to say this."

He set his coffee cup down and looked at her anxiously.

"Yes," she said eventually.

He grinned from ear to ear. "Great! That's fantastic! I'll let Nelson know right away so he can get all the details taken care of for you. I'll give you his number. Please call him this morning. He'll want to get all your information, and you need to tell him what kind of car you want so he can have it delivered today. Oh! You'll need to go shopping and get some new clothes…" He looked at her work outfit and then looked back at her eyes. "Uh, all new clothes. You have to look the part of a billionaire's girlfriend, and stop by the salon, too, please. Get your hair done, nails, the works. I'll give you an extra allowance for that, that's all so you can fit the job description, so I'll pay for all of that."

She giggled and smiled at him, finally, and he smiled back at her.

"This means you'll have to date me quite a bit over the next couple of months, so that people believe us when we get married," he said in a hushed voice.

"I can't believe I'm doing this," she said with a slow shake of her head.

He shook his head as well and whispered to her, "Me either. I've never had to pay a woman to date me before."

She rolled her eyes and wrote her number down on a piece of paper, then slid it over to Peter. "Here. Give this to Nelson and have him call me. I have to go back to work."

Peter looked at her in horror. "No, you don't!" he said unapologetically.

“Yes, I do. I have to tender my resignation.” She smiled at him, and then turned and walked out of the door.

He sank down in his chair and finished his coffee, not entirely sure that he was making the right choice, but hoping that it was just what his life needed to be turned around. Then he called Nelson and broke the news to him.

Chapter2

Emmaline spent the next week in a flurry of activity. It began with quitting her job and walking out of the sweet little restaurant in the Quarter, and then meeting Nelson. He was incredibly efficient and she was quite impressed with him. He called her within fifteen minutes of her newfound freedom, and he was in the quarter to pick her up in Peter's limousine within twenty minutes. He took her to the bank first and opened some accounts in her name, making enormous deposits in them and while she was signing paperwork and finalizing her new accounts, he was on the phone arranging to have the car she wanted delivered to the house that afternoon.

The rest of that day and several days after that as well, were filled with shopping for new clothes, going for hair and nail appointments, spa treatments, and furniture shopping for her new room at his enormous house. His house was one of the biggest mansions in the city, and it was nestled on a quiet street in an older neighborhood; it was a grand old masterpiece with wooden floors and tall wide windows. There was a beautiful courtyard and an indoor and outdoor pool that were connected and partially covered by a sliding wall of glass.

There were big old gardens with huge towering trees and flowers blooming all over everything that nature touched. The courtyard was lit with hanging strings of soft lights and old fashioned wrought iron gas street lamps that gave off a warm glow. It surprised her because none of it seemed like him at all. She had expected a playboy's lair, but what she found was a southern boy's traditional home in paradise.

She didn't see much of Peter in the first week, he was working on business plans and projects and he knocked on her door and poked his head in twice to see that she was doing well and to ask her if she needed anything. She said she was doing really well and he smiled and went on his way. She decided that if things stayed the way they were, then three years would go by fast and she could by her own sweet little home somewhere in the city.

At the beginning of the second week, he called her and asked if they could sit down together to schedule some dates and she met him in his office with her calendar. They looked at their free time and filled it all in with lunches and dinners at their favorite restaurants, concerts, movies, live theatre shows, and in no time, they were looking at a date for their wedding. They agreed on a date two months away from then and after they entered it into their calendars, Pete looked up at Emmaline and raised his eyebrows.

"I never asked you what kind of wedding you'd like. I was going to suggest that we elope and just make it simple and easy, but we really have to play this out for the press. We have to have a big to-do. What do you want?" he asked, leaving it entirely up to her.

She smiled and looked away for a moment and then looked back at him. "Well, to tell you the truth, I've always wanted one of the big weddings at the church. We could see if we can get married at

Jackson Square and then have a big jazz band lead our guests in a parade through the Quarter."

He grinned at her. "That's absolutely perfect! That's exactly what the press will want to eat up, and then everyone can see how much I adore you, and how reformed I am, and then we will get to work on saving the city."

"Just don't hit on any of my bridesmaids," she teased him with a little smile.

He pushed his mouth out in a very serious expression and tapped his fingers over his tablet dramatically.

"…no…hitting…on…the…bridesmaids…" Then he looked up at her and raised an eyebrow. "Do you have a sister? Is she off limits, too? Or can I have a chance at her? What about a maiden aunt?"

Emmaline grabbed a pillow from the sofa in his office and threw it at him, and he pretended to fall off the desk he was sitting on. "Man down! Man down!" he hollered.

Then he sat back on his desk again and looked at her. "On a more serious note, you said you just have your grandfather left, isn't that right? Would he be giving you away?"

The bright smile faded from her rosy lips and she looked down. "Yes," she said in a quiet voice. "I'll have to go talk to him and let him know I'm getting married."

Peter bit his lip and looked at her in concern. "What's the matter?"

Emmaline sighed and sat on the sofa. "It's just that I thought that he'd be giving me away at my real wedding. I was only going to get married once, to the man of my dreams, and it was going to be perfect and beautiful, and my grandfather was going to give me away. He's not going to live forever, and that was going to be a special memory that we made together, and I have always looked forward to it since I was a little girl, and now I'm getting married, but it's a lie. It's not the real thing. I'm building a fake memory with him. It just hurts my heart." She gave him a sad smile and stood up., "I better go. I'll see you tomorrow for our date." She turned and walked out of the office and went back to her room.

Peter watched her go and felt like he should hug her, because her sadness made him sad, and he realized that she was giving up quite a bit to help him with all that he was doing. It touched his heart in a place where nothing had ever touched his heart before, and it was strange and worrying for him.

The next day, Emmaline and Peter strolled down Decatur Street; her hand tucked into his arm, and him with his hand over hers. She had been quiet since her mention of her grandfather and Peter had been mulling the situation over in his mind. His first order of business was to make her smile.

"I think we ought to start this thing off properly, New Orleans style," he said, looking at her with a sidelong glance and a smirk.

She raised one eyebrow at him and asked, "Really? And how are we going to do that?"

He grinned at her, "Well, with beignets and coffee, of course." He walked her into Café du Monde and they sat at a little table right in the middle of the restaurant. Their beignets were delivered hot to their table a few minutes later, covered in thick mounds of white powdered sugar.

Peter picked up the little dish of pastries and took a deep breath, the blasted it out across the plate, blowing a thick white cloud of powdered sugar all over Emmaline. Then he set the plate down on the table and looked at her and laughed richly. She blinked at him and wiped the powder from her face, glaring at him.

"Hey, now, don't be mad. That's a New Orleans tradition, my dear. Also, I owed you for the water you threw on me. We're even now." He held his hands up to her in defense, still laughing at her, and then he pulled some of the napkins from the dispenser and handed them to her. "Here you go, see if you can wipe that up a bit. Be glad you didn't wear black today." She began to laugh at him and they finally settled down into their beignets and coffee, and the people around them who were locals stared in shock.

When they had finished at du Monde, Peter walked with her past Jackson Square and said in a quiet voice, "I thought we could go meet your grandfather, if you don't mind. No matter if you tell him the truth or if he thinks we are going to get married for real, he will probably want to know who you are hanging around with."

She felt a tear come to her eye and she wiped it away quickly, "That's really thoughtful of you, Peter. You don't have to do that for me, but I appreciate it."

"I know," he said lightly. "But all the same, it's the right thing to do, and that is what I'm working hard on now, doing the right thing."

Emmaline smiled at him and she turned them to walk down Royal. "I'm telling him the truth. I never lie to my grandparents," she said quietly. "I just hope he isn't disappointed in me."

Peter patted her hand and said seriously, "Emma, I don't think anyone could ever be disappointed in you. Not if they really know you."

She glanced at him when he spoke her name in such a familiar way, and she didn't say anything. She decided that she liked the way it sounded. They walked a long way and just as he was about to mention that he could have the car pick them up,

Emmaline turned down a few more streets and then they were standing in front of a little old house with a deep front porch. On the porch, rocking back and forth in his chair like he had all the time in the world, was Emmaline's grandfather.

She walked up the steps and hugged him tight and kissed his cheek. "Hello Papa, how are you today?"

He smiled at her like the sun had just come out and warmed him from the cold night. "There's my girl! I'm good now that you're here. How's my little one?" His eyes crinkled as he looked at her.

"I'm good, Papa. There's someone here I want you to meet. This is my friend, Peter. Peter, this is my grandfather, Henri."

Peter stepped up, pulled his cap off of his head, and waited while her grandfather pushed himself up out of the rocking chair and stood up as tall as he could. The old man looked Peter in the eyes and then reached for his hand. "Hello Peter, welcome to my home. Please have a seat and make yourself comfortable."

Peter shook his hand and then sat down in a chair near Henri. “Thank you, sir,” he said humbly.

“Can I offer you a refreshment? Lemonade? Sweet Tea?” Henri asked, still standing before him.

Peter smiled and was about to decline when he saw the look on Emmaline’s face and he changed his mind at the last moment. “Uh, yes, sir. Sweet tea would be very nice, thank you.”

The old man smiled and nodded, then shuffled off inside the house, humming to himself, and the screen door slapped shut behind him.

Emmaline smiled at Peter. “He just loves company. Thank you for letting him treat you.”

Peter nodded and smiled, turning his cap over and over in his hands. He stared hard at it, and kept silent. When Henri returned, he handed Peter a tall glass with fresh ice and dark sweet tea in it. Peter sipped it and raised his eyebrows, impressed with the drink.

“That’s really good! Thank you so much, sir,” Peter said with a smile. Henri grinned and nodded and sat down.

“I make good sweet tea,” he said as he sat. He got comfortable again and then looked at Peter. “So you’re seeing my granddaughter?” he asked amiably.

“Yes, sir, I am,” Peter answered.

“Well, young man, you’ve got your hands full then. She’s a firecracker. Where’ve you taken her?” Henri looked at him with wise old eyes and a kind smile.

Peter almost choked on his tea, “She and I were at Café du Monde just a while ago.”

Henri looked at his granddaughter’s clothes smudged with powdered sugar. “Yes. I can see that,” he said, stifling a good laugh. “She let you get away with that? She must like you, then.”

Peter smiled and then laughed. “That’s the first time she’s let me get away with anything at all, so I’m counting myself lucky, sir.”

Henri laughed at him. Emmaline moved her seat next to her grandfather’s and took his hand in hers.

“Papa,” she said softly. “I hope you won’t be upset with me, but I want to tell you what it is that’s going on here. You know you’re the most important person in my life and I would never keep anything from you, so I want you to know this, but you can't tell anyone."

Henri looked at her with great concern, but he listened quietly to everything she had to say, occasionally shooting dark looks of uncertainty over to Peter, but he let her finish and by the time she was done with her story, he whistled and leaned back in his chair, then began to rock in it quietly for a long while.

Emmaline waited for him to respond, so Peter followed her lead, and he waited as well and sipped his sweet tea.

At long last, Henri spoke. He looked at Peter. "Why did you choose my granddaughter for this deal of yours?"

Peter looked right at him. "I chose her because she is the most upstanding, honest, hardworking, respectable woman I know, and she is genuinely interested in helping her community. Besides that, she is a truly beautiful woman and she will make a believable wife."

Henri nodded his head and sighed. “Well, I don’t think it’s right, but I understand what you are doing. I’m never going to let my little one down, so I’ll be right there to give you away, Emma, but I hope someday you will let me give you away to a real husband who will love you all of your life like your grandmother loved me. I was a lucky man to get her and I don’t know how I ever talked her into marrying me, but I’m grateful every day that she did, and I want that same kind of love for you, little one.”

She hugged him tight around his neck and then sat back down again and wiped tears from her eyes. He looked once more at Peter. “You better take good care of her,” he said. It was clear that it wasn’t a request.

Peter nodded. “Yes, sir, I will do that. I give you my word.”

Henri nodded back. “Good.”

They stayed and talked with Henri through the early afternoon, and then after Emmaline had washed the sugar off of her clothes, they left him and headed out for their dinner date. Peter hired a carriage to take them through the Quarter for an evening ride and they sat together in the warm air as twilight started to descend and the stars came out one by one.

"You know," Peter said as they rode along quietly, "I really like your grandfather. No one has ever treated me with such genuine respect before. That was a first. You're a lucky lady to have him in your life."

"I know it," she said, smiling, and held his hand as the carriage rolled on.

They spent every day together having lunch and dinner out in town, making sure they were seen by everyone, and all the looks of disgust and disdain began to quiet and calm over the weeks, and they noticed a subtle change in the way that people looked at Peter, and the way they treated him. Peter made sure that Henri went out to dinner with them on Sunday nights, and he got to love the weekly visits with him. Their conversations ranged over a wide array of topics, and none of them were ever boring.

Emmaline had learned that Peter worked in his office in the mornings, and she left him to it, often doing laps in the pool or making breakfast for herself and Nelson and Peter, when they emerged from the war cave, as Nelson sometimes called it.

She was making French press coffee one morning, three weeks into their deal, when Nelson slipped into the kitchen looking more than a little askew.

"What's going on in there today? Are you alright?" she asked him, slightly concerned.

He shook his head and looked longingly at the coffee she was pouring into her cup. "No, it's not going well at all."

She saw his face and handed him the cup of coffee, which he took gratefully. "We're really struggling with part of the refurbishment in the plans. There's a business associate from out of town who is in there right now, and we just can't seem to reach terms on anything. It's warm and tense in there, and I just had to break out to come grab some coffee before one of them kills the other one."

Emmaline nodded and patted him on the shoulder. Then she made a pretty tray, laying out a linen cloth on it, adding a small vase of fresh cut flowers she had chosen from the garden that morning, she placed a plate of cookies and a bowl of wrapped chocolates on the tray and then pulled a pitcher of sweet tea from the refrigerator and nudged Nelson.

"Alright, I'm armed, let's go," she said conspiratorially.

They walked into the office together and she set the tray down on Peter's desk. He looked up at her, in a bad mood and she saw irritation flit across his perfect looking face. She turned her eyes to his business associate who was standing at another table in the office, looking at designs sitting on the surface of it. He was tall and seemingly built of solid muscle. He had jet black hair and light blue eyes. His extraordinary good looks caught her off guard for a moment and she blinked at him and then smiled. He smiled back at her warmly and looked at the tray in gratitude. He walked around the desk, his eyes never leaving her, and he reached for her hand.

"Hello, I'm Tristan." He kissed the back of her hand slowly and delicately, and then released it, his eyes watching her still as she smiled widely at him. "That looks so good. I think it's just what we needed," he said softly, glancing for a moment at the tray. "Thank you for bringing that in."

She shrugged and smiled, but before she could answer, Peter stood up and slammed his hands down on the desk. "No, that is not just what we needed! What we need is a resolution to your stubborn attitude! We can't move forward until you agree with me! I don't think cookies and tea are going to fix that!" He raised his voice and Tristan winked at Emmaline and turned to Peter.

"Sweet tea might sweeten your disposition and your short-sightedness. Can I offer you a glass of it?" His voice was deep and calm, and his tone was polite.

Emmaline wandered over to the table and looked down at the plans. A cursory glance gave her a fair idea of what they were looking at.

"Tea is not going to fix this!" Peter snapped.

Emmaline looked up at them both, and they were both watching her. "What seems to be the hold up?" she asked.

Tristan walked over to the table and stood near her. "I'm sorry I didn't get your name before," he said with a smile.

"I'm Emmaline," she replied and he bowed his head slightly to her.

"Well, Emmaline, we are working on these plans to refurbish a section of the French Quarter and some of the Uptown area and the city here and here as well. Part of our work includes the merger of two businesses, and the challenge seems to be that we are experiencing some legal constraints due to…" he glanced at Peter and then back at Emmaline, "some red tape at the Governor's office that we can't seem to get through. Not all of the legal channels we need to use are open to us because some of the people working on the project aren't, let's just say, favored. So that's holding us up, and while we are working through that, our timelines are being delayed which is holding back the progress of combining the companies. The employees are very concerned about their jobs and future of the businesses and the merger and some of them are talking about leaving for more solid employment. We don't want to lose the talent we have, and legally, we have to keep both companies active until the legal channels are cleared for the merger, so we are stuck about what to do with it with the employees. We'll get through the red tape eventually, but we can't lose our staff."

Emmaline looked at the documents spread across the table and her eyes fell on a map of the Quarter. "Well, actually, it seems like you already have a really simple solution to the whole problem," she said with a smile at Tristan.

Peter stalked over to the table and flung his hands up in the air at her. "There's nothing simple about it! Nothing at all! What do you know anyway? You're just a waitress!"

Emmaline's heart felt like it stopped in her chest and her eyes stung with tears as she stared at Peter's angry face. Tristan placed his hand lightly on her shoulder and looked directly at her.

"What is it that you thought might work for this? I'd love to know. Fresh eyes can usually see things that tired eyes can't." He gave her an encouraging smile and she took a deep breath to steady herself, then she looked at Tristan alone and placed her hand on one of the squares of property.

"This building right here is already refurbished. It's been repaired. Everything in it works. I know the man who owns this building. He rents it out on weekends to local artists for them to show their work in, but it's empty during the week. You could reinforce the confidence in your employees if you move the people from both companies into this one building so that they can work together and move toward combining the businesses. Leave both of the individual businesses operational for the time being so that you meet the legal requirements you have before the merger is done, but just move the staff to this location. They can work together until you get the merger complete, and then you can move them into the building you have for the new company." She looked pointedly at Peter. "Sort of a temporary marriage until the deal is done and then they can go where they are supposed to be."

Both men looked at the property and then at Emmaline in utter surprise. Tristan clasped her arm and shook her hand. "Well, that's brilliant! I never would have thought of that, but then I don't know the Quarter as well as you do, I'm sure. Thank you so much! Peter, what do you think? Would you be willing to do that?"

Peter knew that what she had said would solve everything they were working on that morning. He felt a heavy pit in his stomach and he looked up at her and nodded quietly.

"Yes, I think that would take care of everything."

She watched him with hurt and angry eyes and then looked away from him and smiled up at Tristan. "Thank you, Tristan, I appreciate your kindness more than you know. It was wonderful to meet you, but I think I should step out and leave you two to the details of your work."

Tristan smiled down at her and took her hand, lifting it to his lips again. "The pleasure is entirely mine, Emmaline. Thank you for bailing us out. We'd never have gotten through it without you, and thank you again for your sweet hospitality. I'll enjoy the refreshments."

They shared a pleasant moment, then she turned and walked from the room. Nelson held the door open for her and smiled apologetically at her as she walked out. She was furious with Peter, and she sent him a text to tell him she was canceling lunch. He didn't respond to her. She was out working in the garden a while later when Nelson approached her with a nervous smile on his face and she saw a moment later that Tristan was a few paces behind him.

"Well! There she is!" Tristan called out happily.

Nelson leaned toward her and said quietly, "He was looking for you and I thought you might be out here. Great job in the war cave today. Peter got your message. He's not happy about it, but he got it."

Nelson left and Tristan walked up to her as she set her shears down and pulled off her gloves.

"Emmaline, I wanted to tell you how impressed I was with you in there today. You showed real courage under fire and that says a lot about your character. You also offered us a simple and brilliant solution to a challenge we couldn't see past, and I wanted to thank you for it. May I take you to lunch, if you don't already have other plans?" Tristan asked, his eyes locked on hers.

She felt butterflies swarm in her and it was an unfamiliar feeling; one that made her feel as though she was glowing, and she liked it.

"Yes, I would be glad to join you for lunch. As it happens, I had a last minute cancellation and I'm free today." He held his arm out to her and she slipped her hand into it.

"Good, you can show me that building in the Quarter that you were talking about. I'd like to see it in person. Of course, we'll do that after lunch." He smiled down at her they walked back into the house.

"I'll just go get cleaned up, and I'll be right back," she said sweetly.

"Take your time," he said in a soft tone.

She felt like she was floating down the hall to her room, and it made her giddy. It seemed like she was fifteen years old with a high school crush. She told herself that she was just being silly and he was only a nice man; a business associate of Peter's, and that was all.

Emmaline slipped on a thin gauzy white summer dress that narrowed at her waist and danced in waves around her calves. She set a white sunhat on her head and walked back down the hall to Tristan.

He brightened when he saw her, and she noticed his lingering glance at her. "You look lovely," he said with a grin, extending his arm for her again. She took it and they walked out of the house to his car.

An hour later they were laughing and talking over lunch, sharing stories and truly enjoying each other's company. He toasted her with champagne and told her how she had saved the jobs of so many people that day.

"You truly are an amazing woman," he said, his eyes focused on her.

The corners of her mouth had been turned up nearly the entire time she was with him that day, and his comment only made her smile again. "Thank you."

He leaned closer to her and spoke softly, "May I ask, and please don't answer if you feel it isn't my business, but what was that comment that Peter made to you earlier about being a waitress? What was he talking about?"

She looked at Tristan and knew that she could not betray Peter, "Well, before I became involved with Peter, I worked as a waitress for a while."

Tristan frowned. "He seemed to use that as an insult for you. It shouldn't be. Servers work harder than most people, I think, and many times they are underappreciated for the service that they provide. It's certainly nothing to be ashamed of, and most assuredly nothing to throw at you as an insult."

Emmaline was quite pleased with Tristan for saying what he did and she grinned at him. "Thank you!" she exclaimed.

They walked to the building she had discussed with them earlier and the man who owned it happened to be there. He saw Emmaline and came right to her, hugging her and patting her back.

“Well hello, young lady! I’m so glad to see you out on this fine day. How are you doing?” he asked with a broad toothy grin.

“Well I’m just fine, Mr. Turner! I’m so pleased to see you! How are you?” she asked, her hand on his arm.

The old man nodded and pushed his hat back on his head. “I’m getting by, missy, gettin’ by.”

“Mr. Turner, I’d like to you to meet Tristan. He’s a friend of mine.” She waited as the men shook hands and greeted each other, and then she continued. “Mr. Turner, I was just telling Tristan this morning about this wonderful old building of yours because he’s in need of one that he can rent out for a few things. I told him he might see you about renting this old place from you for a short while.”

The old man looked carefully at Tristan and said, “You’re looking for a place to rent?”

Tristan nodded. “Yes, sir, we are. We need a little spot to set up some desks and run an office for a little while, maybe a few months. This is just the right location, and I like the look of it, Mr. Turner, you’ve really fixed this place up nicely. I'll tell you what, if you'd be willing to rent this to us, I'll pay you whatever your asking price is for a six month lease, and I'm fairly certain we'll be out of here before the six months is over, but you are welcome to keep the full six months payment. How would that be?" he asked hopefully.

Mr. Turner rubbed his hand over his chin and looked at Tristan, and then at the building. Then he turned and looked at Emmaline. "Miss Emmaline," he said quietly, "do you think I ought to lease my building out to this man?"

She took his hand in hers. "Yes, sir, I do."

He nodded. "Alright then, Tristan, the building is yours. I'll be here tomorrow and you can drop the payment off and I'll give you the keys."

Tristan blinked in surprise. "Well, certainly! I'll be sure to be here early tomorrow morning. Thank you, Mr. Turner!" They shook hands and as Tristan was walking Emmaline away, Mr. Turner called out, "Tell your grandfather I'll be by to see him in a few days! We'll go fishing!"

"Yes, sir, Mr. Turner!" she called back with a wave, turning to Tristan with a smile.

Tristan placed his hand over hers and held it snugly. "I am just so impressed with you! I can't believe how easy that was! I've never had a business transaction go that smoothly before! Thank you so much Miss Emmaline!" He grinned at her and they laughed as they strolled down the street.

He had her back at Peter's house a little later that afternoon, and he thanked her wholeheartedly again when he dropped her off. He honked and waved good-bye and she went inside the house, happy as she could be.

She was curled up outside in the garden, swinging on the hanging bench with a book in her hands, enjoying a cool breeze just as the last light of afternoon was beginning to wane when Peter came out to her and, by the look of his walk, she could tell right away that he had been drinking some.

Emmaline looked up at him and saw right away that he was in a foul mood. She set her book down and stood up, facing him, but she didn't say anything.

She knew what was coming, and she had to mentally prepare.

"Well, well, well, there she is, folks. The wonder woman who saved the day," he said sarcastically as he tipped his glass back and swallowed what was left of the contents of it. Then he looked at her and raised his eyebrows in mock surprise.

"I guess our dinner date was off too, then. You never said anything about that. You must really be put out with me for insulting you with the truth today," he snapped at her and took a step toward her.

"Guess what," he said, setting his empty glass on the little table near the swing. "I just got off of the phone with Tristan. He can't stop going on and on about you. He was just soooooo impressed with you today, and do you know what he told me?" He took another step toward her and laughed sarcastically. "He told me that the two of you went to lunch together. Yeah. The two of you, all alone at lunch. Then he said that you walked him over to that building you were talking about this morning and in the snap of finger, you had the owner eating out of your hand and he just gave the building to Tristan for six months so we could move everyone into it like you said this morning."

She moved to take a step back to walk away before she said something stupid, but he reached for her and slid his hand around her waist and pulled her toward him. "Do you know what else he told me? He told me how beautiful you are, and how fascinating you are. What did you two do today, anyway? Huh? Did you tell him that you are my fiancée? Did you? No. You want to know how I know that? Because I thanked him for complimenting me on my fiancée, and he had no idea we were engaged. He congratulated me, and told me what a lucky sonofabitch I am to have you." He looked down at her beautiful face, her dark eyes, her little rounded nose, and then his gaze fell on her full lips. "But I don't have you, do I, Emmaline, because you are out running around with my business partner on a lunch date. I wanted to come out here and remind you that you are *mine*, Emmaline, you are going to be *my* wife and you are not going to go date other men, especially business associates of mine."

She furrowed her brow at him. "It wasn't a date, Peter. I didn't do anything wrong today, and as a matter of fact, I saved your butt in that office today, even after you insulted me, and yes, it was an insult, you said it in a mean way and you hurt me, Peter." She looked at him angrily and he blinked at her for a moment.

"I hurt *you*, today? Well, let me make it up to you, baby," he pulled her to him suddenly, holding her firmly and grasping her face in his other hand as planted his mouth on hers, kissing her hard and hungrily. Her mouth was soft and sweet, and as soon as he did it, he regretted it. He knew he never should have done it. Hers was a mouth that his had no business tasting; his mouth was for women who partied, who drank and lied and kissed many men, women whose mouths were not tender and precious like hers was. He found himself lost in it for an eternal moment, deeply regretting ever having touched his lips to hers, but knowing that they had never tasted anything like the ambrosia of her lips, he knew that he would probably never taste them again, and for that reason, he lingered through the regret for as long as the moment lasted, until the kiss was broken.

Emmaline was too shocked to move at first, and her heart seemed to stop right then. She had been hurt but that had given way to anger and just as she was going to push him away, she felt his kiss change from one of possessive ownership to the gentleness of a boy's very first kiss, and it caught her off guard. His mouth then simply caressed hers, as though he was drinking her in, and she could not move for a moment, though his grip on her lightened to a feather touch.

She felt her heart begin to beat again and she opened her eyes and instinctively shoved him away from her. He didn't fight her and when her hand flew up and slapped his face, she felt the sting of it in her own heart, just as much as he did on his cheek. He looked away from her and said quietly, "I'm so sorry.

I never should have yelled at you this morning, and I had no business kissing you just now."

Emmaline's heart began to race and frustration flooded through her. The pain she had felt that morning returned and the indignation of him forcing a drunken kiss on her was more than she was willing to put up with from him.

"You disgust me," she said quietly, and then she turned and walked from the garden and locked herself in her bedroom.

It was three days before she agreed to see him, and when she did he was sober, clean shaven, and extremely polite. He talked with her in the sitting room and they sat opposite each other in an awkward silence as he raked his hand through his golden hair and she twitched her foot anxiously.

"I owe you far more than an apology, Emmaline. I'm so very sorry for the disrespect I've shown you today and any other day. I never meant to do anything of the kind. I hold you in such high regard, not that you'd know that from the way I've behaved, but I've come to see you as a friend, and I don't have many friends, as I've said, so I'm not willing to lose this bond we have built. It means too much to me. Please accept my apology." He looked at her earnestly and she felt all the irritation and frustration in her dissolve.

"Don't ever treat me like that again," she said resolutely.

"You have my word," he said quietly, "and as a way of making it up to you, I bought you your engagement ring." He pulled a box from a little blue bag beside his feet and opened it for her. Inside was a stunning diamond ring set in platinum.

She gasped and took the box from his hands, looking at it with wide eyes. "Peter, you didn't need to do this!" she said in shock.

He smiled at her. "I did need to do that. It's the least I can do to make up for being a class-A jerk to you. Also, our wedding needs to be believable, and no one is going to believe that someone as flashy as me is going to put a chip of a diamond on my fiancée's hand."

She laughed at him and it felt good to have the tension between them gone. Her friend was back and they were alright again. She pulled the ring from the box and slid it on her finger. “It fits!” she beamed at him.

“Well, yes. I think there is not one piece of information that Nelson didn’t get about you. I have a complete dossier. Ask me what bus you rode in elementary school.”

She laughed again, and then he handed the little blue bag to her. “There’s a wedding gift from me to you in there as well.” He said quietly and smiled at her.

She lowered her eyebrow at him and opened the bag. Inside she found a delicate diamond necklace with a heart on it, and a matching bracelet. “This is so sweet, Peter, thank you!” She moved over to sit beside him and give him a big hug. It was the first time she had ever hugged him and at first he was very careful with her, but then he felt the goodness of it, and he wrapped his arms around her and hugged her back.

"You are so welcome. You've definitely earned it. By the way," he said, letting her go and leaning back into the sofa, "you can keep the ring when we get divorced. It looks good on your hand."

She laughed at him again and held her hand up so they could both get a good look at it. "You know," he said with a slight frown, "I've never liked a girl enough to give her diamonds before."

"Well, consider them part of my retirement plan as your dedicated employee. How about that?" she teased him.

He smiled. "That works."

Chapter3

With the dust from their fight settled, Emmaline and Peter began dating again and made their engagement public. The newspapers and magazines, both in print and online, had a field day with the news, and though they originally started reporting it as a gamble of a marriage, it wasn't long before so many images and stories of them around town together started producing new articles that were written with more of a love theme than a gambling joke theme. By the time the day of the wedding rolled around, everyone in the community was excited for it and looking forward to the big event. They were the "It Couple" of the year.

Peter's indiscretion had been all but forgotten and he knew that he owed all of it to the beautiful woman who was always by his side in public. He took her to a wedding breakfast feast at a special restaurant the morning of their wedding and on their way to the restaurant, he sat beside her in the car and watched her. She seemed to be glowing with happiness, as though she was radiating sunshine.

"You look wonderful today, Emma. I'm relieved to see you so happy today. It makes me think this won't be the worst day of your life."

"Of course it isn't the worst day of my life, why would you say that?" she asked giving him a look as though he were ridiculous.

"Well, I remember what you said about wanting your grandfather to walk you down the aisle when you married for love. I know how important that is to you. Today isn't about love, today is a lie to trick the public and make them think I'm not a complete jerk."

She shot him a low brow look and said, "You are being completely ridiculous. You aren't a complete jerk, and it's time the rest of the world knew it. I wish you liked yourself better. You're not nearly as bad as you think you are." She fluffed her dress and looked at him kindly. "Besides, today isn't a complete lie. I'm marrying a really good friend, and in three years when we get divorced, I'll be divorcing a really good friend, so it's not as cold and heartless as you make it out to be. Now, enjoy it and have fun."

Enjoy it and have fun, he thought to himself, looking at her as she emerged from the car into the bright early summer sun in her stunning wedding gown. It was strapless with a sweetheart neckline that clung to her curves and flared out at the knee in dazzling waves. He tried to stop himself from thinking that he wouldn't be unzipping her out of that dress later that night, and having a real honeymoon. He had had to stop those thoughts more than once in the last few weeks before the wedding. It always made him feel ashamed when they crossed his mind, and he did his best to ignore them when they came, but then she leaned over and hugged him, kissing his cheek as cameras flashed around them and as his face neared the curve where her neck met her shoulder, he breathed in her scent and felt the soft warmth of her skin, and it mesmerized him for a moment.

Go on, he thought to himself, go with your friend and have breakfast.

They sat down with their wedding party and her grandfather at the breakfast feast and enjoyed themselves as they laughed and ate, toasted each other with champagne and then headed toward the massive church at Jackson Square. Tourists and locals alike packed around them and cheered as they entered the church together and before he let go of her, Peter looked down and said, “Emma, you look absolutely stunning, and I am one lucky man. Also, I just want to warn you ahead of time, I’m going to kiss you when the preacher tells me to, so please don’t slap me this time.” He winked at her and she gasped at him in mock shock, then he hugged her and kissed her cheek and walked down the aisle, leaving her at the front of the church with her grandfather.

Henri placed his hands on his granddaughter’s face and said softly, “I wish that this was your real wedding day my little one. You look so beautiful and so happy. I only want a love for you that will last all of your days, and someday, I hope you find the right man to share that love with, but until then, I think you have found a friend that will take good care of you, and that’s enough for now. I don’t think this is a mistake, my Emma, I think you made the right choice to do this. I love you, my girl.” A few tears fell from his face and she wiped them away. “I just wish your grandmother could have lived to see you today, she would be so proud of you, all grown up like you are. I know she’s watching over you from heaven, though, so if you feel a raindrop on your cheek, I’m sure it’s from her.” He smiled broadly at her and she hugged him tightly.

The music began to play and her eyes widened, and a feeling of unease hit her right in her stomach and zoomed through her. Her grandfather patted her hand. “That’s alright, Emma, that’ll go away soon enough.” He winked at her and they started down the long aisle together, passing friends they had known all their lives, who all smiled at her and wiped tears of joy from their cheeks. Partway down the aisle she passed Tristan, who winked at her and her heart gave a little flutter. She took a deep breath and smiled back at him, and then she reached the front of the church where Peter was waiting breathlessly for her.

He had watched her walking down the aisle to him and with every step, he could only tell himself how lucky he was to have her in his life in any capacity that she was willing to be with him in. Her dark caramel skin glowed warmly against the bright white dress that hugged her body as she moved toward him, and her veil could not quite hide her eyes and smile as she reached him and he lifted it over her head. The music stilled and an excited hush fell over the church.

"Who gives this woman to be wed?" the preacher asked.

Henri lifted Emmaline's hand and placed it delicately into Peter's, looking from her to him in all seriousness. "Her grandmother and I do," he said as firmly as he could, and then he kissed her cheek and as he turned away from her to sit down, he wiped another tear from his eye.

The pastor read through the vows, and they repeated promises of everlasting love and devotion to each other, no matter the circumstances, trials or tribulations, and after the promises were made, they both slid rings onto each other's fingers. Even though she knew it wasn't a real wedding, even though she knew they would be getting divorced in three years' time, she could not stop the swell of emotion that rose up in her and spilled lightly down her cheeks.

Peter touched her tears away gently with his fingertips and smiled at her, gazing down at her with his brilliant dark green eyes, and she lost herself in them for a moment before returning her attention to the pastor and his sermon about the importance of keeping their promise and loving one's partner, no matter what, for all the days of one's life.

After what seemed like a surreal length of time, the pastor smiled at them both, pronounced them man and wife, and then told Peter that he could kiss his bride. He had been waiting for the moment. He had wanted it, and he had dreaded it. He knew that it would only happen once, for many reasons. He was only going to marry once, because after their marriage ended, he would never marry another woman again, and also because this kiss would be the only one of its kind in that he had the freedom to kiss her any way he liked for as long as he liked, because they had to sell it to the public.

He felt like it was a second chance at a first kiss, a way to make it up to her that he had fouled up their first kiss in the garden. This was his chance to get it right and make it count, and the pressure of this moment that he knew was coming had been weighing on him heavily.

Peter looked down at her as she smiled up at him, her dark brown eyes alight with happiness, her scintillating smile reflecting all the happiness within her, her soft full lips colored in warm rose red tones, and he promised himself that he would always remember every single part of this moment. There was a hush in the room, and the ceiling fans whirred above them, everyone was watching and waiting as he placed his hands carefully on her cheeks and lifted her face to meet his. He had wondered if he would close his eyes or not, and he was torn between watching this moment so that he never forgot what it looked like when he kissed her, and closing his eyes so he could feel it in all its beauty and wonder. It might be his last chance.

His eyes stayed open until his lips touched hers, and at the first touch, he closed them. He wanted to lose himself in her kiss again, for as long as he could. Peter pressed his lips against her gently, softly, as he breathed in the scent of her and felt the smooth warmth of her dark skin beneath his fingers. He felt her fingers touching his as she rested her hands on his; they were cool and light. The taste of her lips was sweet and as intoxicating to him as the fragrance of a rose. He cared not what anyone else thought, as this was his only chance. He opened her mouth with his and as their tongues met for the first time, he felt a surge of electricity move through him and touch every part of his body, stealing away his breath and pulling him to her as though she was the center of gravity for the whole universe.

Peter's hands moved from her face and slid around her waist, pulling her to him as his kiss deepened, and his entire world began to feel as though it was spinning, and to his amazement, she kissed him back. She kissed him with every bit of passion that he gave her, and she never showed any sign of surprise at his boldness with her. As his mouth moved over hers and he held her tightly to him, he slowly became aware that there was cheering around them, and it seemed to grow louder as he came back to the reality that was his.

He didn't want to let go of her, to stop his kiss, but he knew that it was time to, and as their kiss came to a close, he opened his eyes and saw her lovely face, and he leaned down to kiss her one last time, gently and sweetly before he let her go and she opened her eyes and blinked at him, breathing in deeply and holding his arms. It was then that he realized he had taken her breath away and she was holding on to him to steady herself. He touched her cheek with his hand, and smiled at her, and then he took a deep breath himself and they turned to face the thunderous applause and cheers of their guests.

They walked hand in hand down the aisle and as they exited the church, their guests all followed them out, each one taking a white handkerchief and following them as the jazz band stepped in line behind them and Emmaline lifted her white parasol high over her head, and Peter donned his top hat. They marched through the French Quarter, the band and the guests trailing along behind them in their own parade of happiness.

When the sunshine touched Peter at the doors of the church, it seemed to him like the spell that had taken hold of him in the church was broken and he was somehow released, feeling more himself than he had during the ceremony, but the power of the kiss they shared haunted the edges of his mind all day as their guests enjoyed a luncheon with them, and a dancing party that lasted long into the night.

At some point near the wee hours between yesterday and tomorrow, Peter stole his new wife away in a car and they left their guests with waves and kisses blown into the wind. The car took them to a yacht that was waiting on the great Mississippi River. They boarded it and the Captain began to sail it to the Bahamas where they were going to honeymoon, or at least have a nice vacation together.

They changed out of their wedding clothes and Peter relaxed on the deck, watching the stars as they shone more and more brightly the further out to sea they sailed. Emmaline joined him after a while and sat beside him, enjoying the feel of the cool air on her skin.

They were silent for a bit, and then she looked at him and said, “Well, it’s official.”

He nodded and laughed a little. “It is. You’re chained to me for three years, and then you get parole.” He winked at her and she nudged him with a chastising smile.

“We were convincing,” she said, looking away from him as she spoke. “I nearly fell for it myself!” she said in a teasing voice.

He looked, but he couldn’t see her face for the dark night around them, and he wished desperately that he could. “Well, I had to make it real. I had to make it count,” he said, wondering what she was really thinking.

“It counted,” was all she said in reply.

He sat there a moment longer with her in silence and then found the courage to say, “Emma, I really appreciate what you did for me today. I realize what a huge sacrifice it is for you, and I want you to know that it isn't going unnoticed."

"You're making a sacrifice as well. No more women for you for a while unless you go out of state to find them. All for the sake of the project you want to do in the city. That's a big sacrifice, too," she stated, giving him the benefit of the doubt.

"That's true, that is a sacrifice." He laughed at her, but then his tone quieted some and he said, "Yours though, seems bigger. I'm sacrificing regular intercourse with women I care nothing about. That's not a big deal. You, you're sacrificing the next three years of your life to live with me as my wife. That's three years that you won't be able to find your own Mr. Right, whoever he might be, and maybe get your own serious relationship going, maybe get engaged for real and get married for love. Perhaps have some children. You're waiting for all of that just to help me out, and that's huge. That's the rest of your life on hold just for me."

"That's a very thoughtful observation, Peter," she said, looking at him in surprise. "I guess it is a big sacrifice when you look at it that way."

He looked over at her nonchalantly and hoped that his question sounded as nonchalant as he wanted it to. "What would your perfect guy be like?"

Her laugh was a little too hollow. "Oh, I don't know. Build him from the ground up?" she asked.

"Yeah, build him from the ground up. Who is he?" Peter asked, grateful that she had put a sort of game-like spin on the subject.

"He's a good man. Generous and kind, with a gentle spirit and a good sense of humor. He's handsome of course," she giggled.

"Of course." He nodded back in agreement.

"He's honest and forthright. He could be evil, but he always chooses to be good. He is gentle and passionate, reliable and responsible. He loves to read and learn, he is a lover of classics and a lover of travel. He is adventurous and free spirited. He is selfless and devoted. He believes in equality for all. He is humble and compassionate, strong and motivated, filled with a passion for life and a passion for me, and more than that, a passion for us and our lives and future. He will never hurt me or break my heart, he will never make me doubt or fear. He will always be there to support and encourage me, to build me up and help give me wings to fly so that I can achieve all my dreams and I will do the same for him in return. He is all of those things, and more than that. He's mine." She was gazing off into the heavens by that point, dreamily talking through the list she had created.

"You know that I meant a real man, right?" Peter said, his heart encased in dejection.

She laughed at him and said, "Oh, and he cooks me breakfast in bed sometimes and rubs my back without my having to ask him to do it."

Peter laughed at her more in defense of himself than in mirth, and said, "Now I know you're dreaming."

Emmaline nudged him with her elbow and said, "Well, you asked, but you're right. I don't know if he exists, but I haven't met him yet, so I'm just going to hold out for him until he comes knocking on my door."

"What if he comes while you are married to me?" he asked. He had to ask. It was a fear that gnawed at him with dull teeth and no lack of appetite.

"Then he'll love me enough to wait for me until my parole, when I can be with him, and he will respect me for my dedication to the commitments I have made," she said resolutely.

"He is a good man, Emma. He's a better man than me. If I found you while you were married to another man, I would steal you away in a minute," he said, thinking momentarily of what it would be like to steal her away from her another man.

"Yeah, I know," she said smartly. "That's what got us into this mess in the first place. Your penchant for stealing women away from their husbands. The difference is, I want a man who would keep me." She nudged him again and then patted his arm. "Well, I'm pretty wiped out. It was a long day." She kissed his cheek and he closed his eyes when she did, living for that brief moment when her lips touched his skin, and her breath warmed his cheek, and then she disappeared below deck and he was left alone with his thoughts, which he told himself was a terrible thing to do to a man.

Her words came back to him and whipped at him like the sails on a boat in the wind. "That's what got us into this mess in the first place…" Him stealing women away from their husbands.

That was what she really thought. She believed she was in a mess that he created, and she was stuck there, helping him until she could get out and leave him hoping to find a better man than him.

She wasn't wrong, he had created the mess. He had slept with another man's wife, albeit it was unknown to him at the time he did it. It hadn't been the first time, though, he reminded himself. He hadn't cared if women were married or not and though it wasn't something he sought out when he looked for women, it wasn't a deterrent for him either.

He thought of the man that she had described. Her ideal man. He was so far from it that there was no hope of him being graded on a curve. He wished like crazy that it didn't matter. He wished that she could see past all of his faults and just want him anyway, just need him somehow, and perhaps even just love him in spite of himself. He let himself wish that more than anything, and he wished it on every star above him in the night sky, but then he promised himself that when the stars faded and the sun rose the next day, he was going to be the devoted, reliable, trustworthy friend that she believed him to be, and he was not going to let her down or hurt her, but rather, lift her up to follow her dreams as she had wanted. She deserved that from him, and much more, and he thought to himself that irony could strike no harder than him finally falling for a woman who not only wanted no romantic relationship with him, but had married him with no intention of ever having a relationship with him beyond that of friendship.

He looked up at the universe above him in misery. He was getting what he deserved, there was no doubt about that.

Below the deck in her private cabin, Emmaline hung her wedding dress up in the closet and sank back into her bed. Here it was, her wedding night, and she had married a man she did not love, a man she was only friends with, who would be divorcing her in three short years, and this was her honeymoon. Sleeping alone in her cabin on a yacht in the middle of the sea. How ironic, she thought. Her mind wandered back over the day. She saw her grandfather, kissing her cheek and wiping tears from his own eyes. She saw herself walking down the aisle at the church and looking over to find Tristan standing there, his beautiful blue eyes locked on her as they always were whenever he was around her, and the feeling of butterflies going wild within her as she looked back at him. She hadn't felt that before, and it filled her with wonder and curiosity.

Then she thought of Peter standing there at the end of the aisle, waiting for her and looking so handsome in his tuxedo. He had the strangest look on his face, as though he was in a trance when he watched her, and she realized that he must have been terrified right out of his mind. The man who was never going to have a serious relationship, standing there tying the knot with her and making a commitment before God and all of their friends that he would be her husband for the rest of her life.

She had come to her own terms with God about her choice in marrying him with every intention of divorcing him in three years. She looked at it as a mission of mercy, and fully expected that for what she was doing for Peter, God could forgive her for lying when she married him.

Then she thought of his kiss. It had sent her reeling in his arms and she had almost lost her balance. If she hadn't held on to him, she was sure she would have hit the floor. She hadn't expected him to kiss her that way. She thought he would kiss her lightly on the mouth and that would be that, but Peter, ever full of surprises, kissed her like she had never been kissed in her life. He had sent waves of heat and electricity through her that could have lit up Atlantic City for a month. His mouth was so tender, so soft on hers, like a pillow, almost, and he had somehow seemed hungry and gentle all at once, and it had sent her spinning. Thinking of it sent ripples of heat through her and she touched her fingers to her mouth, and for a moment, closed her eyes as the memory of his tongue tasting hers flooded her mind. She wasn't expecting that at all, and when he opened her mouth and tasted her, it was as though there was suddenly no one else around them. Not just no one else in the church, but no one else anywhere at all, in existence, and her connection to him was the only tether that kept her from flying away. Strong, passionate, gentle, like an anchor that barely held her, but held her with no possibility of letting go.

She felt herself being rocked to sleep in the cabin, and her eyes did not open back up, but rather, she drifted into a deep sleep where dreams of him hovered around her all through the night, and in her dreams, there was darkness, and nothing could save her but his kiss and his arms, holding on to her and wrapping her tightly in the light of his love.

*

Chapter4

Peter and Emmaline enjoyed a long cruise on their honeymoon yacht. They saw several islands and enjoyed watching multitudes of sea creatures. Their island paradise excursions gave them adventures that they loved and new experiences in unfamiliar cultures. It also gave them time to talk and get to know one another on a more personal level that they had not reached before. After all, they had been strangers in an arranged marriage. It was time for them to become friends.

A conversation they had shared on their wedding night as the yacht left New Orleans and headed out to sea had rattled around the back of Peter's mind and he kept thinking that he would bring it back up to talk with her about it more in depth, but he had not found the right time and place to do it until they were lounging at a private house they had rented on one of the islands. It was surrounded by jungle vegetation and the luxurious house had been built around a warm natural spring that came up to the deck at the back of it, lapping gently and providing background noise.

Peter had gone out onto the deck late one afternoon and found Emmaline swimming in the spring. He watched her quietly for a length of time before she saw him, and when she did, he waved and walked out to the edge of the deck where it stopped over the water.

"How is the water?" he asked with a smile.

She swam to him, serene and blissful. "It's incredible," she said lightly. "You should try it out."

"Alright," he agreed, standing up and stripping down to boxers, then jumping into it and splashing everything in sight. She howled and laughed at him, and when he swam up to her, she raked her hand across the top of the calmed water and sprayed him with a huge splash of it. “Payback!” she called out and he answered her challenge with an all-out water war.

Half an hour later, they were both exhausted and he called a truce and went to rest beside her at the bank of the pool. They laughed at one another and she watched him with guarded trust.

Peter looked at her bright smile and sparkling eyes and had to look away so that he didn’t reach out to her and pull her to him to kiss her soundly. He took a deep breath and said nonchalantly, “Well, it might not be a proper honeymoon, but it’s certainly been a fun vacation. I think we both needed this, there’s been a lot of tension lately.”

"Well, that'll change now that the wedding is over and the city is starting to look at you with new eyes. Did you see all the pictures and articles online?" She was incredulous at the amount of press coverage their pseudo-wedding had received.

"I saw a lot of it. Nelson has been keeping me updated through emails and calls. It looks like our charade is working. I owe you more than I can ever repay you, Emma." He turned to look at her again, and she shrugged.

"You are paying me for it though," she said with a tilt of her head and a small smile.

He looked away again. "I know. I just don't think there's any way I could ever even the score with you. You really saved me and my business. Now that my reputation is at the precipice of a better day, I'll be able to do the refurbishments in and near the French

Quarter that I've wanted to do and get that project going. It's going to take some more time and a lot of work, but I feel like we at least have a chance now, and I owe that all to you. I just wish there was something I could do to really show you my gratitude. Something that isn't just money. You have changed everything, in more ways than one."

"I'm being paid for it. I'm not a saint, Peter." She looked sidelong at him and leaned her head backward, closing her eyes.

He looked at her, watching her for a moment and then moved closer to her and said more softly, "You gave up any chance that you might have at real love for the next three years. If that's not sacrifice, then I don't know what is." Peter was a lot of things, but he knew how much love could mean.

Emmaline's eyes remained closed and she replied, "Not really. There's no telling if or when I will ever meet him. He may not show up in my life till long after we've gotten divorced and gone our separate ways. You might not be keeping me from him at all. We won't know till my dream guy finds me."

Peter thought back over their conversation on their wedding night. "That was quite a list of qualifications you compiled for him. I'm not sure you're ever going to find him. I've never met a real man like that."

She laughed at him. "Maybe that's because birds of a feather often flock together." Her mirth sounded in her again, and she continued, "Besides, we don't have to worry about you finding him or meeting him. I need to be the one who finds him, or be looking in case he's trying to find me."

Peter watched her laying there in the water, her head back and her hair wavering gently in the ripples that played with it. He looked at her mouth and thought of the kiss they had shared at their wedding. Their only real kiss, as he didn't count the time he had planted his lips on hers in a drunken act of idiocy. He wanted very much to lean over her and kiss her again, but part of him railed against it just as much as part of him desired to do it.

"What if your perfect guy is just a little bit different than you think he will be?" he asked, finally giving voice to the thoughts that had reached their tendrils from the back of his mind and tickled the curiosity of his conscious thought.

She spread her arms slightly, moving them back and forth in the water as if they were wings that would carry her through it. His eyes moved from her lips to the swelled curve of her breasts and then he looked away from her and took a deep breath, trying to refocus his mind.

"He'll be exactly what I think he should be or he won't be my perfect guy. I'm not really asking for that much. He'd be a pretty decent man. That's not out of the question. If he's not a pretty decent man, then he doesn't need to be with me." She felt it was quite simple, and she genuinely didn't think she was asking for too much. She knew what she wanted, and she wasn't going to settle.

Emmaline had a point, Peter thought. It just precluded him from being anywhere near the picture.

He was quiet for a long while and then said, "Well, it's getting late. We should go in for dinner. I'm sure they'll have it served up for us pretty soon." He swam back to the dock and she followed him.

When they got to it, he turned for a moment to watch her swim to him, and when she reached him she wrapped her arms around his neck and hugged him, and then she kissed his cheek.

"Thank you for taking me on this trip. I've never seen anything so incredible in my life as the things we've seen while we have been traveling. You didn't have to do this. It's not a real honeymoon, but you made it almost as good as one anyway. I appreciate that." Her voice was soft in his ear and her breath caressed his skin. He slid his arms around her and pulled her to him to hug her back and as he held her there in the water, their skin touching the full length of each other's bodies for the first time. He felt a force of desire go through him that he had never known and it stopped him completely. He did not breathe and he did not move, because he knew if he did, he would not have the will to hold his desire back, and his need for her would cause him more problems than he had ever known.

Emmaline felt his body stiffen when she pulled herself to him in the embrace, and though his arms went around her and he held her to him, he seemed to freeze where he was, half of his body pressed against hers, their arms around each other and his face turned away over her shoulder. She realized that he must feel extraordinarily awkward having her so close when they were supposed to be business associates. She had thought that after their wedding, after the powerful kiss he had shared with her when they spoke their vows that some of the walls between them had come down, but that was apparently not the case. He could not have been less receptive of her friendly affection to him and it was a sharp reminder to her that she needed to keep her distance from him, no matter how comfortable he made her feel, and no matter how amiable he had been with her.

She let go of him and backed away, putting a distance of a few feet between them, and he breathed out slowly and then turned from her and climbed out of the water onto the deck. He reached behind him to help her out, and she waved his hand away.

"That's alright; I can get it on my own. Thanks, though," she said, trying to right the faux pas she had obviously made with him and give him the space he clearly wanted.

Peter knew that he had gone too far with her when she wouldn't let him help her out of the water, and he forced a light smile and replied airily, "Okay, well I will see you inside for dinner then."

They ate their meal with only some light banter shared between the two of them, and afterward, they both retired to their separate rooms, each one of them pushing the other from their minds.

There were moments during their trip when they seemed to be able to be friends, and there were moments when the air between them was filled with awkward tension. Emmaline thought it was the growing pains of getting to know someone who had suddenly become a permanent part of her life, while Peter chalked it up to having to control his lust for her. He had never been turned down by any woman; they had always come to him in constant waves, and he had never found himself without one wanting him, and he had never had to be alone with just one that he couldn't have. It was very frustrating for him.

There were women who flirted with him in places where they saw people as they went along their trip, but Emmaline either didn't notice or she didn't care, and that frustrated Peter. He knew full well that it shouldn't bother him that she didn't want him, and especially that she hadn't paid any attention to the subtle flirting of other women along the way, but all of it began to wear on him tremendously. It was tiring for him to be friends with her and want her, but not be able to have her, and then to not have other women as well.

By the time their trip ended and they returned to the house, he was feeling petulant and irritable, and Emmaline ignored it and stayed in her room and in areas of the house that he did not frequent.

It was when she had embraced him in the spring pool and he had frozen stiff in her arms that she realized how opposed he was to being close to her, and after that, she made it a priority to give him space and turn a blind eye when other women were affectionate and attentive toward him while they were traveling. That one moment, and a few other awkward moments after it, had shown her quite plainly that he meant for them to have a business relationship and a friendly acquaintance, and that would be as far as their friendship would grow.

She had begun to wonder if they were going to become good friends, but then it occurred to her that the weeks leading up to her wedding were filled with social dates because they needed to convince the public that he was through with his playboy days and had settled down into a respectable lifestyle. She understood that she had begun to believe their public façade after all the lunches and dinners out, the movies, the live theatre shows, the concerts, the strolls through the French Quarter, and the boat rides and carriage rides; all of it had only been for show, and it was hard to compartmentalize that into a part of her life where she didn't allow real emotion. It was difficult to remember that everything he did was part of the story they were feeding others. She had decided to keep to herself at the house and give him the space that he had shown her he needed.

In the days that followed the trip, she began to miss being around him a bit, and she decided that it was because she had no company but her own at the house, and that in order to fill that void, she would should join some social groups in the city as his wife so that she could spend her time doing good works in his name.

Emmaline was dressed in a thin summer dress one afternoon and was headed out of the door to go to a meeting with one of the groups, when Peter happened to see her in the foyer and stopped her.

“Well hello, stranger!” he smiled at her. He walked up to her and couldn’t decide how to greet her, so he settled on a light hug. “I haven’t seen you much lately. I was wondering if we could have dinner tonight,” he asked, his heart beginning to pound. He tried to keep his eyes in contact with hers, but the temptation was too strong to resist and as she glanced away for a moment, he let his eyes slide down the curves of her body. He could see the outline of her form through the light material of the dress as the sunlight from the front windows silhouetted her. It made him catch his breath and he turned and looked away from her.

Emmaline looked down to check her phone to see what time the meeting ended and when she looked back up, his head was turned and his gaze was on something else. He didn't look back at her right away when she began to speak, and she knew that he must have only asked her about dinner to be polite. She thought she would give him an easy out so that he wouldn't feel obligated to spend time with her.

"Oh, I wish I could. I have a meeting in the city and I'm not sure how long it will run. Please go on ahead without me. Thank you, though," she replied with a smile.

A brush off. She had given him another brush off. He felt like it was all that she was doing since they came back from the trip. The frustration in him began to bubble to the surface and he stalked into the bar near the drawing room and poured himself a shot of whiskey. By the time he had finished his third shot, he had begun to convince himself that he was doing just fine without any affection or attention from her, and that he didn't need it at all anyway. He called up a couple of the girlfriends that he used to see from time to time and had his limousine go pick them up and bring them to the house. By the time they got there, he was buzzing and happy on the surface and bubbling with resentment deep underneath. He decided to throw a party for the three of them. He decided he'd show her that he didn't need her.

Amy and Tiffany showed up half an hour later and came into the drawing room in happy surprise. Amy rushed up to Peter, her long blonde wavy hair swinging around her shoulders, and she tackled him in a hug, Tiffany, her dark curls bouncing as she joined them, added to the group hug.

"It's been so long since we saw you! I thought you forgot about us, and then you got married! Where's your wife?" Amy asked conspiratorially.

"She's out on the town tonight, so I thought we'd have a little party here, and you two don't need to worry about her at all." He walked over to the stereo and cranked the music up full blast. The girls whooped and hollered and he gave both of them a drink and tossed their coats in the corner.

Peter felt adrenaline pumping through him, and the feeling of freedom and abandon that used to arouse him so much and make him feel alive began to course through him. He grinned in pleasure as he grabbed Amy and pulled her into his arms, holding her close to him and in a flash, he planted his lips on hers and ravaged her mouth in a hungry, lustful kiss. She gasped and moaned happily and kissed him back just as voraciously.

He felt as though he was suddenly himself again and it felt so good to him. “God, baby, you don’t know how much I needed that. I feel like I’ve been on a desert island and I just got back to reality! Oh! Come here, Tiffany, show me how much you missed me.”

Tiffany grinned and looked up at him through her dark eyelashes. She moved up close to him and began to rub the front of her body against his, flirting and smiling as her hands closed over his hips and she squeezed him tight.

Peter laughed and tipped the bottle of booze in his hand back, pouring it into his mouth. Then he tipped it back over Tiffany’s mouth and poured quite a bit into her. Then he set the bottle down beside him and kissed Tiffany; he kissed her hard and long, nibbling and biting at her, and she giggled.

"Peter! Look how much I missed you!" Amy said as she began to dance for him seductively, smiling up at him and twisting her body around as she slowly unbuttoned her top.

He raised his eyebrows. "Oh! I like that! That's going to make me feel so much better."

Tiffany grinned at him and said, "I can make you feel so much better, too, honey." She unbuckled his pants and dropped them to the floor, then pushed him down onto the sofa and lowered her glossy red lips to his groin. His smile stretched all the way across his face as she pulled his shirt off and began to run her tongue over his growing erection.

Amy's shirt fell to the floor and her dance became much more erotic as she smiled at them and slowly peeled off more of her clothes, stopping only to suck down large quantities of booze.

Peter watched them both, looking from one to the other as Amy danced and Tiffany moved her tongue and her mouth over his thick, solid desire. He drained the last of his bottle and set it on the table beside him, then he reached his hands down and knotted his fingers in Tiffany's dark curls, clenching her head and drawing her face closer to his body, pushing himself further into her mouth and throat. He pumped his hips toward her face slowly, enjoying every single second of his pleasure and the magnetic attention of the girls.

Amy had gotten down to her bra and panties and came around behind the sofa he was on, tilted his head backward and leaned over his face from behind him. He let go of Tiffany's head as she sucked hard at him and reached up behind him to pull Amy's bra off of her. He flung it to some corner of the room and buried his face in her generous breasts, devouring her nipples as his hands clenched her swells. She grinned at him and ran her hands over his bare chest as he continued to pump his erection into Tiffany's mouth.

He was lost in pleasure and in lust, enjoying every single nuance of it, of the two beautiful women who had come when he called them and who he knew loved to play with him, and even in the tawdry depths that he was in, Emmaline somehow wound up on the edges of his thoughts. She seemed to be watching him disapprovingly from the corners of his mind, and it began to eat away at him, until he had grown frustrated with her again, and he knew he had to try to drive her even further from his mind.

He let go of Amy and focused with laser beam intensity on Tiffany, clasping her head again, and pushing himself into her hot mouth faster and faster, until his body finally gave him what he wanted and he came hard, filling her mouth and flooding her throat. She squealed with delight and he kissed her forehead and then pulled Amy down onto the couch with him and yanked her panties from her body. He pushed her legs apart and buried his face between her thighs, covering the outside of her with his tongue, and then driving it into her, drinking her in, flicking his tongue over and around her as she moaned and cried out in pleasure.

Peter tried his best to keep Emmaline from his thoughts, thinking that the more he tasted Amy, the more he licked and sucked at her, the more he could push Emmaline from his mind, but the further he went with Tiffany and Amy, the more she came into his thoughts, until he was rock hard again and the only thing he could think of was the wife he could not take to his bed.

He could not hold himself back from his thoughts of Emmaline, from imaginings of her laying on the couch with him rather than Amy, pretending that it was her body that he was giving so much pleasure to, and that it was her cries that were sounding in his ears and her dark hands that were twisting desperately in his blonde hair. He closed his eyes and moved above Amy, covering her nipple with his desperately hungry mouth. Behind his closed eyes, it was Emmaline's nipple being toyed with by his tongue and caught in his teeth. It was her fleshy dark breast in his grasp, and it was her body that he thrust his solid erection into, feeling her hot wet body close around him.

He gasped and began to move within Amy, almost believing his fantasy, feeling her legs tighten around him as he buried himself in her narrow depths. Pleasure washed over him as he pretended it was her voice calling out his name and crying out in orgasm after orgasm as he slid himself in and out of her. He held her tightly and let his emotions change from the petulant, "I'm going to show her that I don't need her," to "She is finally mine and I can have her and make love to her like I've wanted to."

His mouth and tongue moved over her nipples and breasts, across her skin and her lips, sucking and biting, tasting and twisting as he pushed himself deeper into her, his hands grasping at her body tightly. His mental release was a huge relief for him, as he made believe he was making love; and the release of his body came much later, as he spent every second he could with his eyes closed and his mouth open on Amy, imagining she was his untouchable wife Emmaline.

He rolled on the couch with her, putting her on top of him and moving her over his groin so aggressively that he finally couldn't hold back his orgasm any longer and in the final throes of passion, he came again, harder than he had in Tiffany's mouth, filling Amy's cavern with his ejaculation, as images of Emmaline coming for him filled his mind, and he cried out in ecstasy just as he heard the door slam and he looked up as his heart pounded in his chest and he tried to catch his breath.

Tiffany sauntered over to him in all of her lovely nudity, and knelt down beside him as he lay there on the sofa with Amy astride his body. Tiffany leaned over him and kissed him long and slow, running her tongue over his and biting his lower lip.

“I think that was your wife, but I’m not sure. I didn’t see her come in here. I just saw someone leave and close the door.” She said with a giggle.

Amy leaned down and tried to kiss him, too, but he turned his head away. There was a black hole in the pit of his stomach and he couldn’t figure out what it was from. Amy rubbed her breasts on his chest, teasing and taunting him until he looked at her and she kissed him, and he let her.

He had no reason not to.

***

Light filtered in through the drawing room window and the music still played as loud as it had the night before when Peter woke up. He looked around and saw that both girls were draped over him and all of them were nude. He was hung over and saw three empty bottles of booze lying around them. It had been a party, alright. He heard a noise and realized that the noise was what woke him up. It was a knock. It was coming from the door of the drawing room.

"What?!" he called out. His head pounded mercilessly and he covered his eyes with his hands.

"I want to talk to you when your guests leave," she said.

His whole body cringed at the sound of the voice. It was ice cold. He opened his eyes and saw Emmaline, standing a few feet away, glaring down at him. He made a quick move to cover himself and discovered that there was no need to cover his lap because Amy's blonde hair was blanketed over him where she had fallen asleep with her face nestled in his groin. He looked up at Emmaline with panicked eyes and his heart felt as though it would beat right out of his chest.

She stared back into his eyes with an icy glare and waited for him to reply.

"Fine." It was all he could say. He felt horrible about having her find him with the women, but he owed her no reason or excuse; after all, they were business partners, and that was it. He felt horrible because he had let his lust for her get the better of him and he had imagined her beneath him, above him, wrapped around him as he moved inside of her, and now she was looking at him and he wanted to turn himself inside out and hide.

He kept an indifferent expression on his face and watched her as she turned and stalked out of the room, slamming the door.

The sound woke both girls and when Amy realized where she was, she giggled and grinned at Peter, then turned her head and began to kiss the tip of him and suck on him gently.

He pushed her away and stood up. “Sorry, baby, I’d love to let you have your way with me, but I guess I have a meeting I have to go to. Shower in the bathroom through those doors and help yourselves to anything in the kitchen.”

Emmaline had heard the music coming from the drawing room when she got back from her meeting and went to see what was happening because it had never happened while she had lived in the house. The drawing room was neutral territory for them, but she tended to stay away from it. When she opened the door, she wished she had stayed away from it. She had gone in and found a brunette woman sitting nude in a leather chair with a bottle of liquor, and Peter on the sofa with a blonde on top of him riding him like she was going to win a rodeo belt for it. She honestly felt like she was going to be sick.

She turned and left without a word, but when Peter hadn't answered her text that morning, she went looking for him and found him with his women at the end of their party. She was livid and hurt, but more than that, she was angry, and he was going to hear everything she had to say.

He walked into his office in a silk robe that was tied at the waist and set a cup of coffee down for her, keeping his own in his hand. "I'm sure you weren't thrilled to walk in on that. I'm sorry you saw it," he said, partly sorry and partly not. There was the smallest fraction of him that felt justified, however, as though letting her see what she was missing out on might show her what she could have had if she had only wanted him like he wanted her. The majority of him was ashamed at what she had seen. He didn't like that she had seen him that way.

"How dare you!" she seethed at him as he looked at her in utter shock. He had never before had to answer to any woman for being with any other women, because he never kept girlfriends or let himself get into a relationship. This was the first time it had happened. "Just…how dare you?"

"How dare I sleep with other women? I'd like to remind you that this marriage is a business arrangement," he said, coolly.

She felt her fury compounding. "No. How dare you throw caution to the wind and gamble everything we've worked for to blow your reputation by screwing a couple of women in our own home! How dare you disrespect everything that I have sacrificed to help you! I have given up living at my home, I gave up my job, I gave up my freedom, I gave up my whole life! Everything! I gave up everything to marry you so that I could help you fix your sullied reputation and enable you to do the work you want to do in this community and what thanks do I get? Right after our highly publicized honeymoon, I get you throwing it all away and sleeping with two women right in our home! How do you think that makes me look?" She raged at him, and he felt his own anger building inside of him.

"So I can't have any women at all now? What am I supposed to do? I can't have…" He had almost said he couldn't have her, but he'd stopped himself just in time. "I can't have what I want, so I just have to do without it all together? What am I going to do, be celibate for the next three years while we are married?" he shot back at her, frustration taking him over.

"No, I don't expect you to do that, you are welcome to go be with anyone you want to be with, be with as many as you want to be with, just don't do it in this state! Don't do it so publicly with women who will spill the beans to the next available reporter! I can't fix your reputation if you're busy running around behind my back destroying it by doing the same things that dragged you down into the mud in the first place! You're totally negating everything I'm doing! If you're going to act like this here, then I don't even see the point of my wasting the next three years here with you, because you're just going to make my time and efforts useless anyway! I don't fight losing battles." She was being very careful about not raising her voice, but it was difficult.

He didn't know why, but he hated her saying that he could be with anyone. It was obvious that she didn't care at all. Peter was completely incensed. "I have treated you like gold since you've been here, I've done everything for you, and worked hard to help you make this arrangement a success, and now I can't even blow off a little steam in my own home!"

She moved toward him in hopes that a closer proximity might somehow help her get her point across to him. "I don't care what you do, or who you do it with, I'm just telling you not to do it where you can be seen! Out of state from now on! I didn't give up everything in my life just so you could make a fool of me! You have said you are grateful for the sacrifices I've made for you and you wish there was some way to pay me back for them, well, this is no way to pay me back for all that I have done for you! Why don't you put someone else besides yourself first, for a change?"

He felt his blood curdle at her words. She was right. He knew she was right. This was no way to repay her and he had said that her sacrifice was something he could never compensate her for. He pressed his lips together and turned away from her.

Peter's voice grew quiet. "Fine, I'll leave the state in the future."

"Good," she answered behind his back, and then as he turned to look at her, he heard the door close and saw that she was gone.

He fully understood now how so many men were in torment about their relationships. How they loved they women they wanted but had such a hard time being with them. This was one of the reasons why he didn't want to be in a relationship. It was so much easier to enjoy them and kiss them goodbye. He sighed heavily and sank down into the seat at his desk. She was complicated and irritating. Confusing and frustrating beyond measure. She was almost indefinable to him.

Emmaline went straight out to the garden and paced through the rows of flowers until she calmed down. He was nothing short of infuriating to her. She couldn't imagine how she had let herself get into such a convoluted mess as she was in now. Her life had been peaceful and beautiful, living with her grandfather. She had a good job, she worked hard, she had no secrets and she was respectable. Somewhere along the line, she had just gone wrong.

Now it seemed to her that her life was inside out and nothing was what it ought to be. She had more secrets now than she ever had and she was stuck in a marriage with a man who was never going to put anyone else before himself. She tried to stop the tears as they rolled down her cheeks, but she couldn't. She wept a while, until she was calmed, and then she watched the sunset and hoped he would keep his word.

Chapter5

Emmaline and Peter didn't see much of each other in the days that followed the fight. Neither one of them really knew what to say to the other, nor did they necessarily want to talk. He was angry and hurt by her cold rejection, and she was frustrated with his thoughtlessness and his selfish actions.

When they did see each other, it was awkward and quiet. She began to wonder when that would change, because she knew that all things do over time, but living practically alone in a huge house was going to be hard on her, and she hoped that they could at least be friends, because three years of solitude would be too much for her to handle well.

Peter was experiencing a phenomenon he had never known before. He was heart hurt over her reaction to him. He had acted out, partly hoping to make her jealous, while hoping to show her that he was just fine with her not wanting him, and hoping to elicit some sort of response from her, some feelings of desire toward him, but none of that happened. All he had managed to do was incur her anger over his selfishness and he felt that all she had seen was his darker side. There was a growing bitterness in him about it.

He was sitting in his office one morning, about a week after it had happened, still fresh and raw in him, when Nelson walked in and Peter snapped at him a few times before Nelson, who had worked with Peter for a long time and knew him fairly well, sat down and asked off-handedly, “How are things going with the city? Are we able to move the project forward at all yet?”

Peter's eyes narrowed. "No. We aren't any further along with the city. They want more meetings, they want more paperwork, and they want more money. They want more time with Tristan to go over everything, and he suggested that I become more of a silent partner for this deal just so we can get it through all the red tape. I accidentally sleep with the Governor's wife once, and this is the hassle I face afterward. Luckily, his re-election campaign is weak and I don't think we'll have him in office much longer. Hopefully his replacement will want to see this refurbishment happen sooner than later."

Nelson watched him and then asked lightly, "How is it going with Emmaline?"

Peter scowled. "Not well at all. She is cold and quiet, she might as well be an ice-queen! I can't believe I married anyone at all, let alone her!"

Nelson took a deep breath and said in a low tone, “Sir, we agreed that she would be a wife in name only and that it would be a business deal. You aren’t talking about physical relations with her, are you?”

Peter caught himself and felt heat flush his face. He turned away from Nelson and focused on the papers laid out across the table he was standing over. He had meant physical relations. He’d been torn over wanting her and feeling angry with her for that need not being reciprocated by her, but it seemed clear that the frost between them was not going to thaw anytime in the future and it weighed on his heart and his mind that she was in the same house, just down the hall, and he could not go to her; he could not touch and have what was not offered to him, but what he wanted so badly. “No, of course not, Nelson,” he lied. “I mean that she and I have our differences of opinion when it comes to my being with other women. I run hot blooded. You know that, she knows that, I think that everyone must know that, but she wants to curtail my physical activity with other women here in my own home, and not only that, here in my own city. In my own state as well! She is insisting that I go out of state anytime I want to indulge in some physical release. I can't go running off to some other state every time I want a woman or two for the night. That's bad for business." He stalked around the table and splayed his hands on the table, looking over the papers there, but not seeing them. "I could have women come right to the house, but she won't hear of it. If I want some company, I have to leave the state for it! When did she assume any kind of authority over my life? When did I allow that to happen?" He grew more irritated speaking his thoughts out loud.

Nelson nodded thoughtfully and walked over to the table, also pretending to look at the papers, but not really seeing them. "Sir, she isn't wrong about that. It would look absolutely horrific for you if you were to have women coming to the house here where your wife is and be caught having an affair with them. Especially because she is so likeable. It's the same in town, if anyone in the city caught you and knew who you were, it would be disastrous. We have our hands full just trying to rectify the damage that was done by your situation with the Governor's wife, but to destroy all that we have managed to rebuild through your marriage by cheating on your wife, at least in the public eye, would be a devastating blow to your reputation that I'm not sure you could recover from."

Peter grew angry. “Well, what am I supposed to do then? Just forgo women unless I happen to be out of town?”

Nelson rubbed his chin. “No, sir, of course not. I could arrange out of town trips for you two or three times a month if you like. It’s just a change of protocol, if you choose to look at it that way.”

“It’s a pain! What in the world ever made me think that getting married would be a good idea? I could have kept my old reputation and lived the way I wanted to for the rest of my life instead of answering to a woman who isn’t even a real wife! I can’t believe I did this! I probably ought to look at having it annulled. What a disaster!” he grumbled loudly.

Nelson shook his head. “Sir, you did it to enable you to move forward with your business plans. It’s much bigger than just you being allowed personal freedom. It's the improvement of the community and the betterment of an area of the city that we all love and that brings enormous tourism in. It's the acquisition of wealth and prosperity."

Peter looked up at Nelson. "I have plenty of wealth and prosperity, Nelson, I'm a billionaire, but you do have a point about the city."

Nelson continued. "If you think broadly about it, sir, you really have the best of both worlds. You have a beautiful, intelligent, kind, and thoughtful public wife who has considerably improved your reputation, and enabled you to further your project more than you could have without her. She has been out working with several programs and groups in the city and your name is shining because of it. You have the ability to go and enjoy other women as often as you like, so long as you do it away from the place you are tidying up, that being your home and your city. It's really not a bad situation, sir. I can arrange to have the jet ready to take you anywhere you'd like to go a few times a month and that may alleviate some of the tension you're feeling. Things are heading in the right direction, and that's just what we want to happen. We shouldn't risk damaging the progress we've made, and we have made some, sir."

Peter knew he was right. He couldn't very well admit that the real rub was that he wasn't able to have Emmaline, the only woman he really wanted, in this state or out of it. He realized that he was probably going to have to make some sacrifices himself and listen to them both. He would have to fly out of the state for personal leave from his marriage. It was ridiculous, but it was the only way it would work, and Nelson was right about the progress they had made.

He couldn't really afford a regression after they had come so far, even though it wasn't far enough. He sighed and sat in the chair at his desk.

"Alright. Figure something out for me. Maybe three day trips, perhaps three times a month. We'll see how that works out. Plan them for states far from Louisiana, though. I can't have locals who may be traveling notice me and come back with tales." He felt defeated and dejected. Sacrifice did not sit well with him, but in the back of his mind he could hear Emmaline's words and his own back to her, and he knew that she was making the same sacrifice, except she wasn't leaving the state for conjugal visits with random lovers, and he was. He hated the guilt that came with feeling selfish; they were emotions he had never felt before and he didn't like them.

"Very good, sir. I'll take care of it and get it arranged for you." Nelson replied.

***

Two weeks later, Emmaline was relaxing in her room when she got a phone call from her grandfather, Henri. She was excited to hear from him until she heard his voice.

Henri sounded weak and tired. "Hello, my baby girl," he said in a thin voice.

She drew her breath in and held it. "What's wrong? You sound like you don't feel too well!" Her hand flew to her heart, and her fingers curled.

"Well, little one, I'm not doing too well. I didn't want to say anything at first, but it's getting worse and I need your help, if you can do it," he said quietly. She knew he would never ask for help unless he really needed it and though she would love to help him with anything, he liked for her to have her own space and freedom. She knew that it must be bad if he had gotten to a point where he was actually asking for help.

"Of course, I'll be right there!" she said and hung up the phone. Her thoughts were a blur as panic rose in her and adrenaline coursed through her veins. She threw several pieces of clothing into a suitcase and some bags and carried them down the hall to the foyer, where she saw Nelson coming out of Peter's office. He took one look at her and rushed to her.

"What's wrong? Where are you going?" he asked with a worried look.

She turned to him as tears began to fill her eyes. "It's my grandfather. He's very sick, he sounded really bad. I have to go to him!"

"I understand, of course." Nelson nodded and picked up her bags. "Let's go. I'll help you out. Stay as long as you need to with him, and don't worry about anything here."

She looked around and then her eyes went back to Nelson again. "Where is Peter?" she asked.

Nelson shifted uncomfortably. "He's ah… he is out of state for a few days. Personal trip."

She realized what he meant and irritation moved through her. Of course he was gone, off to some other state, sleeping with any number of strange women, when she really could have used the support. Emmaline sighed and nodded, then walked out of the front door and closed it behind her, feeling like she was closing the door on all her emotions for Peter; both the good and the bad. They loaded her bags into the car and she drove to her grandfather's house. She found him lying in his bed, sleeping. She sat in his room with him until he woke up and saw her there. He smiled widely at her with tears in his eyes. "Thank you so much for coming," he said softly.

She rushed to him and hugged him tightly. "Of course, I love you so much. There is nowhere else I would rather be." She kissed his cheek and touched his forehead. It was burning with fever.

"Don't you think we ought to get you to the hospital? You need to see a doctor," she said in a quiet tone.

He shook his head. "No, I can't go to the doctor. I can't afford it, baby. I can't afford the doctor or the medicine. I'm old anyhow, and I have been missing your grandmother so much. If it's my time to go, then so be it. I'll go this way and then I'll be back with her. I only wish I wasn't leaving you behind. You really are the only thing keeping me here." He touched her face and smiled at her weakly.

The panic in her came back and flooded her whole body. Sorrow clutched at her heart with its icy fingers. "Grandfather, no! You can't do that. Please let me get a doctor for you. I'll take care of the bills. You won't have to worry about any of that. You won't have to worry about anything!" she pleaded, holding his hands in hers.

He closed his eyes and shook his head. "No, I won't have you spending money like that on me. You just stay here with me for the time we have and that will be enough for me." The words came slowly from him as he struggled through speaking them to her.

Emmaline felt as though her heart might be ripped out of her chest as she watched him trying to rest and fight off his illness at the same time. She spent hours with him, holding his hand, talking to him when he was awake about memories that they shared, and alternately pacing and sitting when he wasn't awake.

Friends of his that regularly came by to see him learned of his poor health and word spread quickly through the quarter and surrounding neighborhoods. People came by to see them both, to bring food and offer comfort and company. Emmaline hadn't felt as much at home as she did in the days that followed her arrival at her grandfather's house. It was so good for her to see people that she knew and loved; people who had seen her grow up and who genuinely cared for her, but somewhere in her heart there was a small hole. She ignored it, but that place that Peter should have filled was left hollow, and it tugged at the corners of her when she wasn't distracted by the people who came by.

All of them asked about Peter, and wondered where he was. She said that he was out of town, couldn't get home right away, and that was all she would say. Everyone focused their attentions on Henri, and hoped that he would improve, but as each day passed, he seemed to get gradually worse, and Emmaline was afraid that his comment about finally getting to see her grandmother may come to pass. It crushed her spirits to think of losing him, and all she did, day and night, was stay by his side.

Mr. Turner, who had leased a building in the Quarter to Peter's business partner, Tristan, came by to see her grandfather.

"I'm so sorry to see him like this, Emmaline, I never thought anything could keep your grandfather down. He's been a strong and resilient one since we were boys. I hope like crazy that he makes it through this alright."

"So do I, Mr. Turner. I don't want to know what I'd do without him." He hugged her and sat with his friend for a while, telling fishing tales and trading smiles, but Henri was very weak, and their visit didn't last very long.

He walked to the door when his visit was over, and looked at Emmaline. "You know, he's always going to be with you, you just might not always be able to see him with your eyes."

"I know. I just prefer to be able to be with him in person, that's all. I don't want to be selfish, but I don't want to let him go." She said as tears rolled down her cheeks. He hugged her gently and she wiped the tears away and smiled at him, "Thank you for coming down, Mr. Turner."

"I'll be back tomorrow to see him. I'll likely wind up wearing out my welcome before this turns one way or the other, but he's one of my oldest friends and he has been there for me through a lifetime of good and bad, so I want to be here for him as well," he said quietly.

Then he tilted his head and looked out of the screen door. "Is that your new husband?" he asked in a hushed tone, pointing his old finger across the street to a long dark car that had pulled up. She looked and tried to hide the shock on her face when she saw Peter step out of the car.

"It is indeed, Mr. Turner," she answered him.

"Well then, I'll leave you two to Henri. Good-night, Miss Emmaline." He hugged her again and walked out of the door. She followed him, but only went as far as the porch where she stayed while Peter crossed the road and nodded at Mr. Turner as he passed him. He came slowly up the steps and stood before her on the porch.

"Nelson told me that you left, he said Henri isn't doing well. I came to see what I could do," he said to her in a soft tone, his eyes meeting hers. When he had come home from his trip and discovered that his wife was gone, he got into the car immediately and went to Henri's. He hadn't felt so worried about another person in a long time, and the unfamiliar sensation compounded the worry that he had for Henri. He felt strange about letting Emmaline know just how worried he was. It was too much like letting down his defenses and letting her in enough that she had the option of hurting him.

She had watched him cross the road in utter surprise, but she didn't show it. She hadn't expected to even hear from him, let alone watch him walk up the steps to her grandfather's house, and there he was, standing before her, offering her his help.

Emmaline shook her head. "He doesn't want the help," she told him.

Peter saw that she was holding back her emotions, and he wasn't sure how to help her, but he knew all the way to the depths of him that it was all he wanted to do. "What's wrong with him?"

"He won't tell me and I'm not sure. He won't go to the doctor. He's worried about the bills that he'll get from the hospital and the medicine he'll need to get better. He won't let me do anything except be here with him and take care of him as best I can at the house." She closed her eyes and tried desperately to hold the tears in, but she couldn't, and when Peter saw the first one fall, he reached his arms around her and pulled her into a strong embrace, holding her tightly against his chest. She had not felt so secure in ages, and in the comfort he gave her, she began to sob and all the emotion in her crashed outward in waves as she let it all go. She breathed him in as she cried, and the scent of him settled her a bit, calming her some, as she released her angst.

He rocked her gently and stroked her hair, and he let himself lower his head and kiss her cheek. “Go ahead and let it all out,” he whispered to her. “It’s going to be alright. We’ll get it taken care of. He hasn’t told me not to help, yet, so I’ll stay out here for a bit and see what I can do. I’m sure I can help you.”

Her tears finally slowed and she took a big breath and let out a sigh that took much of her grief with it. He gently wiped her tears dry with his fingertips and lifted her face to look up into his. He hated seeing her so distraught, and he was going to go to every length to make sure that it would all work out. He also hated that he hadn't been there from the beginning, as he knew this had been welling up for days.

"I'm going to do everything I can. It'll be alright," he told her and as she looked up into his beautiful face and saw that he was in earnest, and she let herself believe him. It was rare that she let anyone do anything for her, but this time, it seemed like he was doing it without asking, without permission, without worrying about whether she would let him or not, or whether he had the right to; he was just going to take care of things and that was all there was to it.

Emmaline looked up at him and felt a surge of gratitude in her heart. His kindness touched her and it was the first warm feeling she'd had toward him since their honeymoon.

He hugged her once more and then let her go and walked the length of the porch to rest on the railing. He pulled out his cell phone and dialed Nelson, telling him to get a physician to the house immediately. Fifteen minutes later, there was a doctor at the door and he was taken in to see Henri.

Henri wasn't happy about it, but when he saw Emmaline's pleading eyes, he relented, and the physician gave him a thorough examination. When the doctor was finished, Peter walked outside with him and Emmaline stayed in the room with her grandfather.

"I told you not to call him," he huffed quietly.

"I didn't call him, Peter did. You didn't tell Peter not to do anything." She smiled at him.

Her grandfather harrumphed once and looked away and then after a long moment, he looked back at her and said, “Well, I guess it’s a good thing he did.”

The doctor walked back into the room and said, “Henri, I have to tell you, if Peter hadn’t called me when he did, you wouldn’t have been here with us by morning. I have a nurse bringing me the medication you need, but this was a close call. You can’t wait so long next time, no matter what, call me, please.”

Emmaline held her breath and didn’t let loose the gasp of horror that choked her. She listened to the doctor tell him what they needed to do to help improve his condition, and then the doctor said that Henri needed his rest. Emmaline kissed her grandfather and they walked out, leaving him to his sleep.

She and Peter thanked the doctor as he left, and then Peter walked out to the porch and sat in the chair beside Henri's rocker. Emmaline walked out of the house and knelt before him on the porch.

"I don't think I could ever thank you enough for what you've done," she said, her heart in her throat, her eyes misting over again. He looked down at her and wanted more than anything to kiss her, but instead he took her face in his hands, leaned forward and brushed his lips on her forehead. He closed his eyes as their skin touched, and he held onto the moment as long as he could, but then he released her and sat up in the chair again.

"There is nothing to pay me back for, Emma. You and he needed help, and I helped. There's nothing more to it than that. You've done so much for me, Emmaline, it's the very least I could do for you." His voice was quiet, but his words were full of meaning and emotion, and none of it was lost on her.

She looked down. “I’m sorry I had to leave the house, and I’ve missed a lot of my meetings and social obligations because of this. I had to come though.”

He shook his head. “Please don’t apologize. He’s your grandfather. Stay as long as you need to, take whatever time you need.” He leaned forward to her and could not hold himself back from taking her lovely face in his hands again and tilting it up so he could look into her eyes. “Just come back home to me as soon as you are able,” he said, and then he leaned in and kissed her cheek softly and gently. His breath on her skin and his kiss sent ripples of electricity through her and she held his hands to steady herself. Her eyes closed and her mouth opened slightly as she tried to catch her breath, but he let go of her, and the sensation was gone. She thought she must be very tired. She hadn't slept much at all since she had been there.

He pulled her to her feet and hugged her close to him. She could smell his scent again; the same sweet smell that had calmed her when she was crying earlier. He rubbed her shoulders for a moment and then let her go. "Let me know how he's doing and if he needs anything at all. I've taken care of the doctor and all the medicine. We just need to keep an eye on him for now, and he should be alright soon. It's just good that we got to him when we did."

"Thank you," she whispered. He smiled down at her and made himself turn to leave. He knew if he didn't turn away from her then, he would not be able to stop himself from kissing her, and that was the last thing either of them needed just then.

She watched him walk across the street and her heart swelled with appreciation for the friendship he had shown her. She felt a new warmth for him that hadn't been there before, and it made her happy.

Through the days that followed, Henri grew healthier and stronger, and two weeks later, he was back out on his front porch again, rocking in the sunshine and trading fishing tales with Mr. Turner. He wasn't quite well enough to go fishing, but he would be soon enough, and it was then that he told Emmaline that it was time to go back to Peter.

"I'm getting along just fine now, my girl, and you have your own life to go live. It's time you went back, before people start talking and say that you left him for good," he told her with a smile.

She had been thinking about it, but she wasn't sure she wanted to leave her grandfather until she knew that he was alright. He seemed to be, so she packed her bags and loaded her car again, and Emmaline went back to Peter's house.

When she came in the front door, Nelson poked his head out of the office door and when he saw her, he came toward her happily. "How is Henri? Is he better? The doctor has been giving us good reports."

He hugged her lightly, and then Peter appeared in the doorway and he and Emmaline smiled widely at each other.

"Look who came home!" he said with a grin. He hadn't realized that he would miss her, but miss her he did, and seeing her standing in the doorway was a welcome sight that warmed his heart and made him feel as though everything in him had suddenly come back to life.

"Hello!" she said happily, and then she turned her gaze to Nelson as Peter walked toward her. "He's doing just fine now, thanks to this guy," she said, as she looked up gratefully at Peter.

He shrugged and gave a humble smile. "I didn't do anything at all. It was the doctor, really. Listen, Nelson and I are just about finished, why don't you unpack and let me know when you're done, and I'll take you to dinner to welcome you home." He looked at her hopefully, and she nodded with a grin.

"Okay. I'll see you in a bit." Peter carried her bags to her room for her and Nelson headed back into the office. It was nice to be back in her room, and somehow it didn't seem as lonely as it had before.

She unpacked and dressed for dinner in a light yellow summer dress. It hugged all her curves and there was just enough material in the flared hem for it to dance a bit as she walked.

She twirled a few times in the mirror and watched the edge of the dress waving and fluttering. She smiled to herself and then jumped when she heard his voice behind her.

“I never could figure out the appeal of turning in front of the mirror until now. You make it seem delightful,” Peter said, standing in her doorway with an amused grin on his face. She gasped and covered her mouth in surprise and he walked in toward her.

“I’m sorry I caught you off guard. I didn’t mean to surprise you, but your door was open.” He smiled at her and nodded. “You look lovely.”

Emmaline felt a flush rising up in her face and she smiled back at him. He nodded to the door. "Are you ready?" She nodded and they walked out of the house for dinner.

He took her to a little restaurant on Royal Street for dinner. "I love Royal," she said.

"I know. You told me once. That's why we're here," he said giving her a sidelong glance.

They sat down to dinner and she looked at him curiously. "I've been gone a while. What's going on with the project down here?"

He rolled his eyes and took a deep breath. "Well, there's a lot going on and there's nothing going on, simultaneously. The things that are happening are slow but they are moving forward. The things that aren't moving forward are because of the Governor blocking me through the city political chains at every opportunity he gets. It's really difficult. One of the things I wanted to tell you is that Tristan will be coming to stay at the house while we work through this. He needs to be here in the city while we get it all together. I am guessing that he will be with us for a couple of months. It really all depends on what happens with the city."

Emmaline listened thoughtfully as he explained more of what was to come.

"I know I got upset about him having lunch with you before, and I apologize for that; I had no business telling you what you ought to do and what you can't do. That's not my place. Also, the guest room he will be staying in is nearer to your side of the house. If that makes you uncomfortable at all, you are welcome to come sleep in my room and I will take the room you're in." He fumbled at the last bit. He was going to say that she could come and stay in his room with him, but then he thought better of it, knowing that it would be too difficult for him if she did, and that it would be inappropriate for their relationship to offer that to her. At the last minute, he slipped in the part about him staying in her room.

She tilted her head and thought about it. "No, I'm sure it will be fine if we are all in our own rooms. We're adults, I'm positive that it won't be an issue at all," she stated very matter-of-factly.

He felt his heart sag a little bit, but kept discussing it with her. "Well, that's good. That's going to be a big help for us in getting this project completed. The Governor is really just giving me such a hard time that Tristan has decided he wants to try and do much of the work in his name so that we can get it all through. The problem with that is that this project has been my baby from the beginning, and he was only supposed to be involved in part of it, but his involvement has expanded to encompass a great deal more than he was ever supposed to be part of. If the Governor wasn't blocking me at every turn, I could get almost the whole thing done myself. I could make the differences in this city that I want to make, and do them in my name, without feeling like my past is constantly being thrown in my face."

Emmaline bit her lip and looked at Peter with a gleam in her eye. "His re-election isn't going very well. He hasn't followed through on his campaign promises from the last election. There may be another excellent solution to this that's a much better and possibly more viable option."

He lowered his brow at her, wondering what he could have missed. "I've been over this time and again in my mind. It's kept me up on several nights. I just can't figure a way out of it. What have I missed?" he asked her.

She turned the corner of her mouth up in a sly smile at him and asked, "Well, what if you ran for governor?"

Peter's jaw fell open. She continued. "Think of it. No one wants to re-elect him, but he's far more qualified than the guy he's running against and no one wants him either, but Governor Collins is the better of two evils. Run against him. You have the monetary means to do it, you are more popular now since the wedding than you ever have been, and you can use your project to refurbish the city as a platform for local community development, and then if you win you won't have any red tape at all."

She sat back in delightful satisfaction and he ran the idea through his mind. It was incredulous.

"You know, that's not a bad idea, but I've never thought of running for office. I've never had an interest in being in politics," he mused.

"You are interested in cleaning up and polishing the city you live in. This is just another way to do it," she said with a smile.

He nodded in deep thought. "I'll talk to Nelson about it and see what he thinks. That's a rather creative solution to the problems. Thank you, Emma." He lifted his drink to hers and they toasted to a fresh start and new ideas.

Their dinner was filled with conversations about what his options might be if he were to take the road she suggested, and they discussed her grandfather and his health. She was so grateful to him for what he had done, she was glad to do whatever she could to repay him for it, and she told him so. If he decided to run a campaign for the Governorship, then she would help him however she could. She pointed out that she was already involved in different community groups and committees, and that her work was being noted around town and published in the papers. She also noted that if he won, a divorce three years into his term wouldn't look bad, especially if she was very clear with the public that it was an amicable divorce and they were going to remain close friends. She would continue to support him and his future endeavors. By the end of the evening, he was nearly talked into it.

Chapter6

Two weeks later, Nelson had jumped onto the Governor's race wagon and their plan was put into action. It became official and Peter was running against the man whose wife he had been caught sleeping with, and who had subsequently stopped most of his business endeavors in the city. It was risky, but it was also incredibly smart.

Thanks to his marriage to Emmaline, his reputation had seen such improvement that the public began to swing heavily to support him in his bid. Photos of him with the Governor's wife were published all over again, and the story was dragged through the mud, but the public had seen it before and they were more interested in his plans for improving the city, and his beautiful new wife who was so involved with the people of New Orleans. After all, if he had improved himself so much, surely he could do the same with the city.

Tristan moved into the house then, and was set up in the bedroom near Emmaline's. He was humble and gracious upon his arrival, thanking them both and getting straight to work with Peter. The first night he was there, they had dinner together in the dining room, and Emmaline was a few minutes late walking in. She looked around and smiled.

"Well this will be a nice change, it's so lovely in here." She sat down and Tristan looked at her with a subtly quizzical look. She saw it and smiled at him.

"We've never eaten in here, or at least, I haven't. I'm just enjoying the opportunity to be able to have a meal in here," she said in an attempt to explain herself.

Tristan looked at Peter and Peter laughed lightly. "Oh, well, usually we eat dinner out," he explained further, wondering why he was explaining himself at all.

They shared a wonderful meal together and afterward, they stood and bid each other good night. Emmaline nodded to both of the men and walked down the hallway to her room. Tristan followed her and she turned to look at him when he spoke to her.

"Oh, Emmaline, please don't feel like you need to take me to my room. It is a big house, but I can find my way." He smiled at her.

She looked at him for a moment and then realized what he must be thinking, and she laughed and smiled back. "I'm sorry, but I'm not walking you to your room, I'm going to my room." She pointed to the door just down the hall. "That's my room." She smiled at him, waved and told him goodnight, and then walked to her room and closed the door as he watched her go.

The next day, Emmaline walked into the kitchen and found Tristan in jeans and a button down shirt. She had never seen him out of a suit, and it surprised her that he was dressed so casually. He was reaching over the stove, which was covered in pans and pots, out of which puffs of steam and delicious scents billowed into the air.

She laughed a little and looked at him. "What are you up to in here?"

He waved at her. "Come see! I've got all kinds of things going on."

Emmaline walked over and stood next to him, looking down at a huge mix of cooking creations. He pointed to the pans and pots as he went along. "This is a fruit compote that I made of fresh fruit I picked from the garden, we have traditional buttermilk biscuits and white gravy to go with them, sausage, bacon, this is my own special crepe mix which is what the fruit compote is for, and this sea salt caramel glaze goes with that. Here. Have a taste." He held out a spoon, his eyes twinkling.

Her eyes were wide, but she opened her mouth as he dipped a spoon into the caramel and filled it, and then lifted it to her waiting lips. The moment it touched her tongue, her eyes closed and she moaned in delight. She smiled and looked up into his sky blue eyes. He laughed a little and reached his fingertip up to her chin, wiping a drip of the caramel off of it and then pausing a moment before slipping his fingertip into his mouth and sucking the sweetness off of it.

"That was my fault," he said. "I spilled a drop on you. It's good though, isn't it?" he asked with a grin.

She felt her breath catch when he touched her, and that, coupled with the sweet caramel she had just swallowed, put an enormous smile on her face. "It's incredible! What are you making all of this for?" she asked.

He shrugged and looked down at all of it. "Well, it's just my way of saying thank you for dinner and for having me here while we work out the business. Besides, I like to cook. Don't you like it when people cook for you?" he asked, with his eyebrows raised.

She nodded. "It's one of my favorite things," she said, thinking that it was also one of the things on her perfect man checklist. She had even shared that one with Peter. She wanted a man who would cook for her without being asked to do it, but she didn't say anything about it to Tristan.

Instead, she looked around and asked, "When will it be ready?"

He turned in a circle, found the stack of plates and handed one to her. "Here you go. It's ready now, so please feel free to dig in!" He watched her as she laughed and loaded her plate with all the delicious food he made, and then she sat at the small table in the kitchen.

He took a step toward her and asked, "Isn't everyone having breakfast together in the dining room?"

She stopped short for a moment and then looked up and him and shook her head. "Oh, I guess one of us should have mentioned something about it to you. We don't really eat together, unless we eat out. Last night was sort of a welcome dinner, I think. We've never eaten together in there. You're welcome to eat anytime you want to and anywhere you want to, but we don't really have sit-down meals with each other."

He stared at her for a moment and then sat down opposite her at the small table, "Well, I like to eat with other people, so if you would do me the honor, I would very much enjoy your company at least at breakfast and dinner here, unless you have other plans. Can I arrange that with you?" he asked with a smile.

She blinked at him for a moment and then smiled back at him. "I'd love that! My grandfather and I used to share all our meals together if we were both home, and I miss it so much! Count me in for sure!"

He smiled and stood up to get himself a plate. She stood up as well and walked over to the electric kettle, turned it on and then pulled her French press from the cupboard.

"Do you like coffee?" she asked.

He smacked his forehead and smiled. "How could I have forgotten that? Yes, I love it! Bit of a necessary evil in my line of work," he said. By the time he was sitting at the table, the coffee was ready and she took it to him.

They enjoyed a delicious breakfast together and as she was helping him clear the dishes away and put the left-over food into the refrigerator, he looked at her and said, "I haven't really seen much of the house. Maybe later today you could give me a tour. What do you think?"

She nodded. "I'd be glad to, although, I think there are places in this house that I haven't even seen yet, and many that I haven't used, so it will be an expedition for both of us!"

He seemed surprised, but he smiled and thanked her, and they went their separate ways. Emmaline went into Peter's office and saw Nelson and Peter looking over the paperwork.

"Good morning!" she said to them. "You just missed an amazing breakfast. Tristan cooked for everyone. I wasn't sure where the both of you were, but there's still some food in the refrigerator if you'd like it."

They both smiled and nodded. "Nelson ate before he came and I had coffee. We're good. We're elbow deep in work here. Is there anything else that you need?" Peter asked with a courteous albeit busy smile.

She walked toward them and said, “I wanted to ask you both something. Our contract for this marriage is for three years, and at the end of the three years I get the money that you’re paying me for being married to you. I just wanted to know if we can take Henri’s medical costs out of that payment.”

Peter stared at her. “What are you talking about?”

Emmaline lifted her chin a bit. “I want to take care of his expenses. It’s my responsibility, not anyone else’s. So I just wanted to say that at the end of three years, instead of giving me three million dollars like we agreed on, just take out all the costs for Henri’s care and give me the difference.”

Peter walked around the table to her, feeling like he had been standing on a rug that she yanked out from beneath him. “Emma, I did that for you both as a gift, please don’t say that you want to pay for it. Let me do that for you, for him, for you both. You have done so much for me, letting me hire you to be my wife and sacrificing your own life to live here and pretend that you're married to me just so we can try to fix my public image, that taking care of that for you and your grandfather would be my honor and privilege. Please, let me do that for you to repay you for all that you've done for me. If you want to, think of it as a perk for being an employee of mine, just let me help you with it, though. I still want to pay you the full sum of money that you'll be earning over the next three years." Peter was nearly pleading with her by the end.

She could see that it meant a great deal to him, and she knew that their original arrangement had changed when he decided to take her advice and run for office. If he won, he would be the Governor and her duties would be significantly increased. "Alright. I'll accept it. Thank you, Peter," she said quietly.

He smiled and nodded and she walked to the door, reaching for the handle, when she realized she hadn't closed it, and when she pulled it open, Tristan was standing in the doorway looking at her in stunned silence. She felt panic rise up in her, and her eyes widened, but he smiled at her and nodded.

"Thanks again for having breakfast with me. I enjoyed it," was all he said, and then he moved aside to let her walk past him before entering the room and closing the door.

She wondered if he had heard anything and decided that he must not have, but that afternoon, she was sitting on the garden bench when he walked out and sat beside her. He approached somewhat slowly, as if he would scare her off.

"Hello!" she said, smiling at him as he handed her a glass of lemonade.

"I took a chance that you like this sweet and sour stuff." He smiled and she took the glass from him.

"I love it," she said with a shy grin, looking into his light blue eyes.

He leaned back into the swing and said, "Nelson and Peter started working on campaign things and I had some free time, since I'm not working on the campaign things, so I came to see if you have a few minutes to talk. I wanted to solve a mystery. See, last night at dinner, you said you hadn't eaten in the dining room together, and I was surprised. Then, when you said good night, you just kind of looked at us both, you didn't touch Peter. You sleep alone in a room on the other end of the house, and then this morning you said you didn't eat any meals together. I was so confused, but then as I was walking into the office this morning, I heard what Peter was saying to you and thought I had better stay outside the office and give you some privacy. I didn't mean to overhear anything, and I didn't know there was anything to be overheard, but…" He looked away and paused a beat, and then looked back at her. "Did I hear him correctly? Did he hire you to be his wife for three years to fix his reputation after that scandal with the Governor's wife?"

She set her book in her lap and sighed. "I'm so sorry you heard all of that."

He nodded. "Well, I saw more of it than I heard. You seem so alone in this big house, like you are trying to fit in and you don't know how to do it. Everything makes sense now, if that's the case and he hired you."

Emmaline covered her mouth to hold back the emotion in her. She felt as if he had stripped her naked in a single glance and she couldn't hide anything at all, most of all her feelings, from him. "You're pretty much right," she said, pressing her fingers to her lips.

She closed her eyes and held back tears as best she could. He slipped his arm around her shoulder and said quietly, "I'm sorry, I didn't mean to pry. I just wondered, after seeing everything, and I felt like I had to ask you. I wouldn't have guessed it. You've really put a good face out there for the public, but where does that leave you here?" he asked placing his finger beneath her chin and lifting her face to see his. "I believed it, when you walked down that aisle looking like the most beautiful thing I have ever seen. I believed you were marrying him, and I wished so hard with all my heart that someday I would find a woman as beautiful and intelligent as you, as sweet and kind, as funny and thoughtful and brilliant as you, to walk down the aisle to me as I waited for her, and I wanted to be so happy for him, for you both, but I was looking at what I wanted. Now I can see that it wasn't true, at least, the tale that was told to the public wasn't true. Now I see that you are more amazing than I ever could have imagined, and you are here in this place, giving your time to him for a price. I have to ask you, is the price of your sacrifice worth what you are giving?"

She stared at him as his words wrapped themselves around her like soft warm petals, covering her in their meanings. Emmaline couldn't even think of a response to what he had said to her, and he saw it. He smiled at her and chuckled.

"I'm sorry, please don't answer that. None of it is my business, really, I just have a bad habit of speaking my mind, no matter what's on my mind. I have been holding a lot of that back, but after what I discovered this morning, it's really been pushing its way to the front of my mind. Please pretend I didn't say any of it." He looked deeply into her eyes and for a moment, she thought he might kiss her, and she drew in her breath trying to steady the butterflies that were spinning in a blizzard inside of her, but he smiled and let go of her chin.

He leaned back against the swing and pushed it with his feet, rocking them both. "Did you know that Nelson and Peter are planning a ball for the campaign?"

She smiled when he said it. "No, I didn't know that! That sounds like fun, when will that be?"

Tristan continued to push the swing, “In about two weeks.” He saw the look of panic on Emmaline’s face and she gasped.

“What’s the matter?” he asked in concern.

“That’s too soon!” she whispered, her warm brown eyes wide.

He furrowed his brow. “Why is that?”

Emmaline looked away from him and said quietly, “I don’t know how to dance. I’m going to have to learn between now and then and two weeks isn’t enough time.” The panic was evident all over her face.

Tristan laughed out loud and let his head fall back a bit in his mirth, and then he touched her shoulder lightly. “I’ll teach you how to dance. We’ll start right now.” He took her book from her lap and set it on the swing, then stood up and held his hand out to her. She was shy for a moment, but then she saw his inviting smile and she slipped her hand into his.

"Alright, but there isn't any music playing." She stood up and he pulled his cell phone from his pocket.

"I've got this," he said. He touched the screen and in no time at all, violins were surrounding them in a forest of notes and sweet moments. He placed his hand on her waist and held his other hand up for her, and she giggled nervously and took it.

"It's just walking gracefully to the notes. I've seen you walk and you will have this down in no time. Step with your right foot, and place it here." He showed her, and she got the first few steps, but then she stepped on his foot and he pretended to be in tremendous pain, falling to the ground, squinting his eyes, and she gasped again, but he laughed at her and stood up to take her into his arms again.

"I'm sorry. I couldn't resist. You're easy to tease and I just love to joke around," he said with a wink. She remembered the list she had rattled off to Peter. She mentally checked off a good sense of humor.

He took her in his arms again and took her a step at a time through the dance until she felt more confident about it, then they stopped and he hugged her, and sat down with her again.

"We'll practice again tomorrow, okay?" he asked. "I'll make sure you are the belle of the ball. I promise. Just save me a dance when we get there, alright?"

She sighed in relief. "That's a deal! Thank you so much."

"Now you just have one thing to worry about," he said with a wink.

She looked confused. "What's that?"

"You have to find a dress that makes you look as stunning as you did on your wedding day. There aren't many dresses out there that would be pretty enough to be worn by you, you see, you'd outshine them too much." He smiled and touched her cheek, then stood up and pushed his fingers into his jean pockets.

Emmaline laughed and looked at him. "Well, thank you," she said with a bright grin. He made her feel so good that she was sure it showed on the outside of her.

"Don't forget, we're having dinner in a bit." He waved and walked back into the house. She watched him go and shook her head, laughing and wondering how it was possible that this beautiful, sweet, funny, charming man had fallen right out of the clear blue sky and landed in her life. Of course he had landed in it right when she had married someone else. The timing of his appearance could not have been more ironic.

She walked into the house and headed for her room. She did not see that Peter had been watching her from the window. He'd been standing there watching her when she was alone, reading her book. He'd been struggling with his feelings for her, wrestling with them, denying them, clinging to his independent and single lifestyle, wishing it was enough for him, but somehow, somewhere deep in him, that belief was beginning to falter, and the more he was around Emmaline, the more he watched her and listened to her and saw her ways, the more he wanted to be closer to her.

He was sitting at the window watching her when he saw Tristan walk out and sit with her, talking to her. He saw Tristan hug her around the shoulders and then make her laugh. He was watching when he saw Tristan stand up and take her hand in his, and then place his hand on her waist and teach her how to dance. He saw Tristan pretend to fall and stand back up, dancing with Emma for a while longer, and then he watched him leave, and all the while, he wished it was him. At the same time, he was glad that it wasn't. He was torn right down the middle about her. He wanted her so badly, but it was a physical lust, a longing to be near her, to touch her, to kiss her, to make love to her, and his heart had begun to bleed into it bit by bit, particularly on his wedding day when he kissed her and then sat out with her underneath the stars as they sailed onto the ocean.

He fought hard to keep his feelings for her as impersonal as he could, but they had begun to become friends, and that was harder to deal with than he thought. He could be closer to her, but not close enough to have her. It was like walking the razor's edge and he wasn't sure where to go with it, or how to do it. He sat there wondering about it, when he felt a touch on his arm, and when he turned to look, she was standing there beside him.

Peter jumped and stood up from his seat on the windowsill. He smiled at her and hugged her in greeting.

"I'm sorry, I didn't mean to disturb you," she said with a smile. "What were you looking at?" She leaned around him to look out of the window in a move to share his view.

"Oh, nothing, I thought I heard a noise, and I was just looking to see what it was. How are you doing?" he asked, thinking to himself that she must be doing very well if she was just coming from dancing in the garden.

"I'm good, but I'm a little surprised," she said. "Tristan just told me that you and Nelson are planning a ball!"

He nodded. "Yes, it's in the works. Two weeks from tomorrow." He felt as though he was giving her cold responses, but he was afraid that if he opened himself up to her too much, he would let his guard down further than he could control, and then he couldn't stop himself from falling further for her. He was sure that it was better to remain cool with her.

"I was just surprised. I don't know how to dance and it doesn't give me much time to learn," she said with a shy smile.

He kept his thoughts to himself, as he cried out in his mind that she seemed to be picking it up pretty quickly with Tristan out in the garden. “Well, maybe you can find someone to give you lessons between now and then,” he said, looking down at his desk.

“Maybe. The other thing is that I will need to find a dress to wear, and I wanted to match what you are wearing, so I thought I would ask you to go shopping with me tomorrow, and we could find something to wear together.” She stepped near to him, looking at him with her warm brown eyes, and he felt his heart tighten in his chest. She reached her hand to him and laid it on his shoulder.

Peter couldn’t breathe. She was so close to him. He could smell the floral scent of her, feel her warmth, and his body responded to her touch. He felt his desire for her growing and it made him flush slightly. He felt like he was a teenager in middle school, unable to control himself. He turned away from her and sat at his desk, moving his chair in close to it. It pained him to admit he couldn't go. "I'm sorry, Emma. I can't go tomorrow. I'm going out of town on personal leave for a few days. Please feel free to get whatever you like, and I will just find something to match it when I get back."

She felt a cold sadness creep up inside her. He was leaving her again for mysterious women in other places. She frowned a little. "Well, I can wait until you get back. What about that?"

He shook his head, not wanting to make her frown even more but knowing he had to be practical. "No, that's alright, go ahead and find something for yourself. I'll shop when I return."

Emmaline felt her heart pinching inside her, and she nodded. "Alright. I'm sure I can find something on my own. Thanks anyway." She turned and began to walk out, but Peter called out to her.

"Emma!" He looked at her earnestly. "I'm really sorry I can't come. I wish that I could. I would like to do that with you, but I just don't want you to have to wait for me. Have a good time tomorrow." He smiled at her and she brightened and smiled back at him.

An hour later, she sat down to a pasta dinner with Tristan. He had prepared all of it and she felt as though she need to say something about that to him.

"You know, Tristan, you don't have to cook every meal. Please don't feel obligated to do that." She winked at him, as he so often did to her.

He nodded. "I know, but I like to cook. It's a creative outlet for me. It lets me try out new things and make mistakes and learn and grow. It's good for me. Speaking of mistakes, did I put too much basil in this?”

She laughed at him and shook her head. “No, it doesn’t have too much basil, but I like basil, so if you think this might be too much, you might want to be careful about who you feed this to in the future.”

He laughed back at her and they enjoyed their dinner together. As they were cleaning the dishes together, he looked at her and said, “I have to go shopping for something to wear to the ball, because, of course, I didn’t travel here with formal wear. I was going to ask Nelson and Peter if they were going anytime soon, but Nelson said that Peter will be gone for the next three or four days. Would you like to come with me, and perhaps we can find a dress for you?”

She remembered what he said about her not finding a dress pretty enough for her to wear, and she smiled to herself. "I suppose it would be helpful to have you there for an opinion. You can tell me what is good enough for me to go home with."

He gave her a sidelong glance and an earnest look. "There's not a dress out there that is good enough to be worn by you, but we'll find something that comes close."

He handed her the towel to dry her hands and she walked down the hall with him toward their bedrooms. They said good night to each other and she slipped into her bedroom and closed the door behind her, her heart fluttering in her chest, as she thought of Tristan. He seemed fun and edgy, unafraid and easy going. He was nice to be around, and as her head touched the pillow and dreams stole her away,

thoughts of him stayed with her through the night.

Chapter 7

Emmaline told Tristan that they were going out for breakfast, but they had a coffee together at the house, and then they set out together and headed into the city to go shopping for formal wear. He took her to breakfast at a little café and she loved it. They talked and joked and then he said, “We need to get my tux first, because I’ll be able to find something quickly and easily. Shopping for you is going to take a while, and with my duds out of the way, we can focus on what you want to wear, which is infinitely more important than what I’m wearing, because everyone will be looking at you, as the potentially new Governor’s wife, and my dear, you need to look the part.” He touched her cheek and lowered his hand, smiling at her.

She hadn't thought of it, but he was right. Everyone would be looking at her, the cameras and lights would be on her, and she would indeed need to look the part. Nothing could be out of place, and everything had to flow perfectly. Her nerves began to burn and she drew her breath in, but Tristan saw her reaction and he took her hand and held it.

"It's going to be okay, Emmaline, you'll be brilliant. You are an intelligent, beautiful, well-spoken woman who loves this city and the people who live in it, and you will shine like the sun before all of them. If Peter wins this election, it will be because you were by his side." He squeezed her hand, and a calmness flowed through her.

She looked at him and smiled in relief. "Thank you so much. I don't know what I would do without you." She meant it, his words had brought her back from the ledge she thought she was on.

Tristan was right; they found his tuxedo in no time at all, and when he walked out of the dressing room and turned slowly for her, she raised her eyebrows at him and grinned. "You shine up pretty nicely!" She didn't want to tell him how beautiful she really thought he looked. He walked up next to her and took her over to the mirror, looking at the two of them side by side, him in his black tuxedo, her in her soft blue sundress.

"Now if I could just find someone even half as incredible as you to have on my arm, I'd be dressed to the nines," he said sweetly. He hugged her shoulder, then let her go and headed back to the dressing room. He emerged in his jeans and button down shirt and she couldn't decide which look she liked better on him, and it made her blush to realize it.

They went to the first dress shop and he looked through the dresses with her, but couldn't find anything he thought she ought to try on. She was curious to know what he thought might work for her, so she let him lead. Two dress stores later, he found a few dresses that he thought might work. He sat by the dressing rooms while she tried them each on in turn and when she walked out, he looked at her from head to toe and examined each dress as though he were searching for the most important thing in the world. The first was a sky blue dress that floated around her like it was made of clouds, the second was a dark green dress that fit all of her curves and flared slightly at the ankles, and the last was a black dress that shimmered when she moved, and was a bit daring in the cut.

She wore each one for him twice as she turned and walked in them, and finally he said, “Would you please put the green dress back on?” She did, and when she walked out, he handed her a pair of shoes that went perfectly with it. “Here, see if these feel alright for you.”

She tried them on and they, like her dress, fit like a glove that was made for her. She looked in the mirror and stared. She had never looked more glamorous in her life, but it was a classy glamour, not a flashy glamour. The dark green satin hugged her body and made her skin glow beautifully. It was like she was wearing an emerald.

He walked up to her and held his hand out for her. “Care to take that dress for a test drive?” he asked with a gleam in his eye.

Emmaline laughed and looked around. No one was watching them. She slid her hand into his and he pulled her closer to him than he had the day before. He began to lead her in a dance, and at first she was self-conscious of the goings on in the store, but in mere moments, she had forgotten everything around her except the feel of him so close to her. She could feel his heat and his body through the fabric of her dress, and it made her catch her breath. Tristan lowered his cheek to meet hers, and his breath caressed her skin. She closed her eyes and breathed in the moment, the feel of him against her and his arms and hands on her. The song playing over the speaker in the store changed and he let her go and stepped away from her.

He was short of breath, but he looked at her and smiled. "That dress is the winner. Do you like it?" he asked, staring at her intensely.

She looked away from him and glanced back into the mirrors. She didn't even feel like it was herself that she was looking back at. "Yes, it's really beautiful."

"Good. Go put your sundress back on and hand this one to me over the door. I'll have them wrap it up for you." He waited as she went back into her dressing room. She took a deep breath and settled the butterflies in her, and then changed back into her sundress.

When she walked to the front of the store, he was waiting for her with bags in his hands and a smile on his face. She tried to pay the clerk and the clerk smiled and shook her head. “It’s already taken care of, ma’am,” she said with a smile.

Emmaline looked at Tristan and gaped in surprise. “Tristan, you don’t need to do that!” He just smiled at her and held the door for her. “Let’s get lunch. I know we’ve both worked up and appetite.”

She thanked him, and they put the bags in the car and walked through the French Quarter as she took him to her favorite place for lunch. They talked and ate, enjoying themselves again as they indulged in true Cajun food. Two hours later, they returned to the house and she took the boxes to her room to put her dress and shoes away, but when she opened the boxes, she discovered that he had bought all three dresses for her, and shoes to go with them. She cried a few tears at his incredible generosity, and in her mind, she checked several more things off of her perfect man list. It was becoming clear to her that he was the best fit for her of any man she had even considered.

Emmaline walked through the house looking for him, but she couldn't find him. She texted him to find out where he was, and he texted her back and told her she had a dance lesson to come to.

She smiled widely to herself and walked out to the garden, only to find herself in complete amazement. The trellises and columns were all wound through with white fairy lights, as were all the bushes and trees. It was like she had walked into an enchanted land. She saw him by the swing, and he stood up and walked toward her, holding a single red rose in his hands. Her heart pounded in her chest and she walked toward him.

He handed her the rose and held out his hand to her. She shook her head. "You are too much. I can't believe you bought all three dresses for me! I thought we were just getting the green one!"

He slipped his hand around her waist and pulled her close to him again, and looked down at her. "Oh, you need to wear the green one to the ball, but the other two look so beautiful on you that we couldn't leave them behind."

She laughed and looked up at him. "Well, thank you, and what happened out here?" She turned and looked in amazement.

"Do you like it?" he asked earnestly.

She nodded. "I love it. I love it so much." Her eyes were shining as she looked at all of the lights and then looked at him. "You are so amazing. Thank you."

He pressed her to him and smiled. “Just like you, so amazing. More than I could ever have guessed. Every time I’m with you, it just seems like I learn more about you that makes me…” He paused and looked down at her. She looked up into his face and he shook his head in wonder and then leaned down to her and pressed his lips softly to hers, kissing her with a tender sweetness that felt like it flooded her with light. His arms both closed around her and his hands closed on her back.

He moved his mouth over hers slowly, softly, taking his time and tasting her, one kiss after another, as though he were savoring every single moment of it, and she felt as though she were made entirely of air, as if the butterflies had finally broken free of their cage inside her and had taken flight, and taken her with them. She moaned softly and his kiss deepened in response, wanting more of her. Tristan held her and kissed her for a long while before he finally let her go and they took a deep breath.

"I'm not going to apologize for that," he said in a whisper. "I've wanted to kiss you since you tried to tell Nelson and Peter your idea and he called you a waitress. There is just so much strength in you. There is more beauty in you than I have ever seen in any woman, and it should be cherished, not bought, not bartered, not taken, nor sold. It should only be given, and only to those whom you choose to give it to. For those reasons, I will not apologize. I know you are married, but in your heart, you are free, and if you want to kiss anyone, then you should be able to. You shouldn't be kept in a cage where you are not able to love when you want to, or when you need to." He lowered his arms from their hold on her and she took another deep breath and stepped back from him.

“I loved your kiss,” she said softly. “I haven’t ever felt like this with anyone, and it’s incredible; you make me feel so good, but I am contracted to Peter. I am married to Peter, and I need to talk with him about what’s happening between us. You’re his business partner, and I have to respect that. I have to balance my priorities between the three of us. I have to be careful with this, as you know. Everyone outside of this house needs to believe that Peter and I are married and in love, and that cover can’t be lost, or we will all lose everything we have sacrificed to get as far as we have. I just need a little time, I need to try to work this out.”

“I can give you all the time you want. I would wait any amount of time for you. Only let me kiss you once more before you go," he said, placing his hands on her cheeks and lifting her face to his. She slid her arms around him and hugged him back as he lowered his mouth to hers and kissed her once more, sending heat and light through her, making her melt into his arms and wish that she could make her time with him at that moment last forever. His soft lips pressed against hers and opened her mouth, tasting her ever so lightly, teasing her, touching her, making her want just a little more of him, as he held her tightly, his hands moving from her face to her waist and her back, holding her against him. He felt so solid, so good pressed to her body, and her mind let her imagine that this kiss could last without end, that she would never have to let him go and feel her lips without his touching them, moving over them, making her want him to never let go.

He did let her go, though, after a long while, and she touched his cheek and turned, walking into the house without a word, leaving him standing in the fairy lights, watching her walk away. She saw him several times over the following days and he was friendly with her, tender and close with her, holding her, hugging her, kissing her cheek, but he told her that he respected what she had asked for, that he knew that there needed to be some semblance to what was happening between them, and that she needed to talk to Peter to figure it all out.

He told her he would wait, and she was so glad to hear it.

***

Peter came home from his time out of town and Emmaline walked into his office to talk with him later in the afternoon of his first day back. He smiled widely when he saw her come in and he hugged her tightly when she walked to him to greet him.

"Did you find a dress?" he asked. "I felt bad that I couldn't go with you."

She nodded and grinned at him. "Yes! Tristan took me shopping and we found a really beautiful gown."

He felt ill when she said that Tristan had taken her, but he hid it so she wouldn't see his jealousy, and instead he said, "Well, would you please put it on and show it to me, so that I can get a good idea of what I should wear so that I look half as good as you will when I stand beside you at that party?" He smiled at her, and she nodded and went to her room, put the dress and shoes on, and then walked back into his office. He looked up at her and his heart stopped in his chest. She was right. It was a beautiful dress.

She saw by the expression on his face that she had affected him, and it warmed her somewhere deep in her stomach to know that. He walked around his desk to her and shook his head.

"You look stunning," he whispered.

She smiled at him and turned in a circle. He walked toward her and held his hand out for her to take. She was surprised, but she slipped her hand into his and he placed his hand on her back, drawing her toward him, and he began to dance with her. She felt the smile slip slightly from her face as he held her so close. His breath touched her cheek and her neck and it heated her in a way that she had never felt before. She felt butterflies with Tristan when she was in his arms, but Peter's embrace sent white heat through her, and it shortened her breath and made her heart almost pound out of her chest. He leaned down and kissed her cheek softly, letting his lips linger on her skin for a long moment before he stepped away from her and went immediately back to his desk and sat again.

His body had reacted to her again and he could not let her see or feel his solid desire for her. He moved his chair closer to his desk and looked at her with an uncomfortable smile. “That is a truly lovely dress. You have excellent taste.”

“Well, to be honest, Tristan chose the dress. I’m glad you like it. Do you think you can get something that matches it?”

Peter cringed inside and smiled at her on the outside. “If you could leave me a small piece of the hem on the inside of the dress, I can take it to a shop and have it matched.”

She nodded at him and wondered at his behavior. "There's something I wanted to talk with you about as well. I hope you understand." She sat down before him, taking care with her dress and looking at him with a warm and happy smile on her face.

"What is it?" he asked, curiosity wrestling with dread and desire in him all at once.

She leaned toward him, her heart in her hands, and told him, "Tristan has taken an interest in me, and I like him as well. We kissed a few days ago, and I stopped it from there, because I wanted to talk with you, I wanted to know what you thought about he and I possibly seeing where our interests might lead. You hired me to be your wife, and that commitment is a priority for me, but things have changed unexpectedly, and now I want to see him romantically; I want to know what might happen with him. I know we laughed and joked about it, but I think he might be my perfect match; you know, my ideal man. I know there's not really anyone who could fit all of the characteristics on my list, but I think he may be the closest I ever get. I will stay married to you, because that's what we agreed, but I thought since you have your out of state arrangement, I wondered if we might work something out for me where I could see him behind closed doors."

Peter felt like he had been gut checked. He had been leaving town, and when he was there he had every intention of finding women to satisfy his urges and physical needs, but even though he had found no end of truly gorgeous women who were anxious to spend the night with him, he hadn't been able to be with them. All he could think of was Emmaline. All he wanted was Emmaline, and no other woman could turn him on enough to reach physical release. He hadn't been doing what she thought he was doing, because his mind was stuck on her. Now here she was, after they had talked about it, and she was interested in Tristan. She was interested in another man who was living under his own roof as his guest and who was his business partner. There would be no way he could avoid seeing the two of them together, just as he had seen them dancing in the garden the day before he left. He was taken aback and struggled to hold his poker face in place. He wanted to grab her and hold her tightly to him. He wanted to tell her that there was no way she could be with another man. He wanted to tell her that she was saturating his dreams and his waking hours, his thoughts and his heart, that she was becoming the object of his desire more than any other woman had ever been and he could no longer fight it like he had been doing. He wanted nothing more than to give in to it and be with her, but she was sitting before him asking him to let her be with one of the two men closest to him.

He rubbed his hand over his chin, trying to hold in all the turmoil twisting within him. Peter shook his head and forced himself to steady his voice. “I realize that he can be very charming, and he is a likeable fellow, but you’ve been here alone, perhaps he is just good company for you and you are misconstruing your feelings for him. Whatever the case may be, with my election coming up, I really don’t feel as though this is the best possible time for you to explore a relationship like that, outside of our marriage, and in our home together. If it got out at all, if somehow a photograph was taken when you didn’t realize it, everything we have worked for would be ruined and destroyed. The project would be scrapped and nothing that we have worked so hard for would come to fruition. I am sorry to ask this, but I'll need to ask you to wait a little while at least. Perhaps until after the election. No matter if I win or lose, we won't be quite as much in the spotlight as we are in the time leading up to it, and that is the most crucial time. Could you please give me until after the election?" He felt horribly guilty and selfish asking her for the time, because he was only partially asking for the stay of execution based on his election. Mostly it was just him giving himself a little time to try to win her for himself, or at least find a way to show her that he was falling in love with her and let her make a choice between the two of them. He had to give himself a chance, somehow, to try to get her to see what he felt, to see how much he needed her.

She nodded. “I understand. I’ll let him know, then, after the election.” She stood up and smiled at him, cutting at his heart as she turned and walked out of the room, and he whispered after her, “I love you.”

Chapter8

Peter's words echoed in her ears. "*Wait until after the election*," he had said, looking as though he was a hollow shell. Emmaline would wait as long as he asked her to, and the election was coming soon enough. It was months away, but she was in the same house with Tristan, and at least they could be around each other and she could get to know him better as time went by.

Hers was the most unusual situation. She was married to Peter, but it was a marriage of convenience. It was a business arrangement. He was a billionaire playboy who had been caught having sex in a hotel room with the current Governor's wife. He was also a local businessman with every intention of completing a project to refurbish and repair part of the French Quarter and the surrounding neighborhoods when tremendous damage had resulted from the last big hurricane that hit New Orleans. Because of his tryst with the Governor's wife, every time he tried to get through the red tape at City Hall to acquire permits and get inspection approvals or make any kind of improvements, he was stopped by dirty politics. In an effort to stem the negative publicity, he hired Emmaline to marry him so that his public image would evolve from that of the local playboy to one of a respectable businessman.

Their agreement was for three years. He would rent her for three million dollars, they would sleep at opposite ends of the house, in separate bedrooms, and only show the faces of a happily married couple to the public, while keeping their lives as their own behind closed doors. The public loved her and bought their story, eating it up like red beans and rice and gumbo, and the politics that held Peter back from his business endeavors with his project seemed to lighten up a bit, but not enough to allow him to make much progress. He had to bring in one of his business partners, Tristan, who was able to get further with the city than Peter was. Emmaline suggested to Peter that he run for the Governor of the state to replace the current Governor who was giving him so much trouble, and he began a campaign, which meant that if he won, she would be the Governor's wife.

Tristan had moved into their home temporarily, to be able to help Peter work on the improvement project in the city. While Tristan was in their home, he began to fall in love with Emmaline. At first, Peter was just jealous, because he had been fighting his own feelings for Emmaline, trying to keep their relationship strictly business as he had promised her, but the more he was around her, the more he fell in love with her. Emmaline had come to him and asked him if she could see Tristan behind closed doors, and Peter had asked her to wait until his political campaign was over and she had agreed, and it was then that Peter, torn that she had asked to see Tristan, had finally admitted to himself that he loved Emmaline, and wanted her. Knowing that her heart was discovering feelings for Tristan made him keep that revelation to himself.

Emmaline knew she had to tell Tristan that they needed to wait, and while part of her was a little relieved because it would give her more time to get to know him better, most of her heart was disappointed to have to wait for him. He made butterflies dance in her stomach and she loved the warm and happy manner that he had, especially with her. She found him in the kitchen the next morning, making coffee for them both, and as she walked up to him, he closed his arms around her in an intimate embrace.

"Good morning," he said softly into her ear, kissing her cheek, and then letting her go.

She smiled a little, and looked down, then looked back up at him. "Tristan, I talked to Peter."

He nodded and waited for her to continue. "He wants us to wait until after the election results before we go any further with this, just in case someone gets a photo or finds out about us or it's leaked somehow. Just as a precaution. There's a lot on the line for all of us right now. I feel like he's right about this."

Tristan reached his hand up and stroked her face, running his thumb over her cheek and his fingers over her hair. "I understand completely. I don't mind waiting for you. It will only make it sweeter when we can be together." He leaned over and kissed her forehead, and she closed her eyes as his lips touched her skin. He kissed her cheek and she smiled, and then he kissed her lips softly, and at first she hesitated, but the warmth of his lips on hers was dizzying and she pressed her lips back against his and kissed him in return. He looked down into her eyes with longing, but then he let her go.

"It's going to be hard to wait, but we can do it," he said, pulling her into his embrace. She closed her eyes and smiled, thinking of how it would be when they could be together. It was so strange to her that she got married to a stranger only to find her true love.

They spent time together, talking, laughing, and sharing stories about themselves with one another during the times when he wasn't working with Peter and Nelson on the project. Days passed and the night of the ball arrived. Emmaline spent the morning at the salon getting her hair and nails done for the event, and the afternoon getting ready. When she walked out to the drawing room to meet the men, they were all ready and waiting for her, and from the look on Peter and Tristan's faces, she knew she looked good. Tristan took a few steps toward her and then stopped himself, as Peter was walking toward her as well, and Emmaline realized that he was remembering that she was married to Peter and this was Peter's big night.

Peter hugged her and kissed her cheek, smiling at her, and then gave her his arm. "Shall we?" he asked, his face glowing with pride and happiness. They went out to the limousine and, in no time at all, they were walking into the ballroom at the hotel. Photographers and media reporters were all over the sidewalk and in the lobby when they arrived, snapping photographs and asking questions. Peter had his arm tight around Emma's waist, holding her close to him. He knew that this night would be one of the best opportunities he would have to be close to her and somehow show her how he felt, maybe try to change her mind about her feelings for Tristan. He had noticed that Tristan kept watching her and trying to be close to her as well, without being obvious or disrespectful. She seemed to be alright with being so close to Peter, and he decided that he would take complete advantage of that, and use the time to try to win her over to him.

Peter had talked to Nelson about what was going on, and had asked him to keep himself between Emmaline and Tristan as much as he could, and to really push the happily married couple image with the press. Nelson, as always, was on top of it.

When the press stopped them at the door asking for photos, Peter turned and faced the cameras; his green eyes sparkling and his smile wide, holding Emma to his side. She waved and smiled, as she should, and then he turned her to him and lifted her chin with his finger, and kissed her softly, his lips molding themselves to hers, and she drew in her breath as his kiss lingered for a long moment before he let her go and smiled down at her, then turned to wave to the reporters before walking into the hotel.

Peter sat at the head table and had Emmaline at his side and Nelson beside her. Tristan was made to sit beside Nelson, just in case. They greeted their guests, hugging and kissing them, shaking hands and thanking everyone for coming. Peter had Emmaline with him the whole time, and he cherished every moment of it, feeling her so near to him. She looked stunning, and it was all he could do to keep his focus on everyone they met. She walked with him to the podium and stood beside him when he spoke to the crowd, talking about what he was going to do to improve the community. He received a huge response, and everyone cheered heartily for him. He was leading in the polls, and it showed in the enthusiasm of the crowd in the ballroom with them.

Emmaline felt the excitement of the crowd and Peter's happiness as it emanated from him. She discovered that she loved being at his side for it, talking with people about what they were going to do, and she really meant every word she said to the people she talked to. She wanted to make a difference in the community as much as Peter did, and together it felt like they could bring about a real change and improve their city and the lives of the people who lived in it. It brought her a sense of purpose and meaning that she had never known before, and she loved it.

Peter walked off the podium and looked at Emmaline with a genuinely happy smile. "Care to dance with your husband?" he asked.

She grinned at him. "I'd love to." He took her hand gently in his and walked out to the floor. Peter slipped his hand around her waist and as he pulled her to him, something in her swelled and she felt light as a feather with him. He looked down at her, gazing into her eyes, and it seemed like everything around them disappeared and it was only the two of them together, turning in each other's arms, and nothing could touch them.

She smiled and said softly, "Your eyes are the color of my dress." She hadn't realized it before, and it was a sweet little nothing that touched her heart; an unplanned connection.

He leaned down close to her ear and said quietly, "Yes, but no one is looking at my eyes tonight, my dear, everyone is completely enchanted with you, including me. You take my breath away."

Peter kissed her cheek softly and turned her in his arms as the music carried them along. She blinked in surprise, but she liked what he said. As the song came to an end, he closed his arms around her and held her to his heart, and as she looked up at him, he bent toward her and pressed his lips to hers softly, in a gentle and tender kiss, and his kiss lingered as he moved his mouth over hers subtly and slowly. Heat emanated from him as they connected, and something deep in her responded to it immediately; the core of her body began to blaze and she felt a magnetic pull to him that was irresistible and powerful. Her hands went to his face and she kissed him back breathlessly.

When he finally let her go, they realized that a wide crowd of people was watching them dance, and that cameras were going off around them. They turned and smiled at the onlookers, and as the music began anew, he kept her close to him and began dancing with her again, subtly teaching her new steps and turns as they moved, and encouraging her.

She loved the feel of the movement, and she realized with complete surprise that she loved being in his strong arms and at the center of his intent gaze. She noticed that he did not look away from her the whole time he was with her on the dance floor. After several songs together with her in his arms, he sighed in disappointment and said, "I think our public is waiting anxiously for us, and I think we have to go answer to them."

They had been wound up in each other long enough in the dim light of the dance floor, and she knew he was right, though she was sorely disappointed that they had to leave their musical dance cocoon. She smiled up at him and he wrapped his arm snugly around her waist and walked with her to the crowds of people waiting for them.

She hadn't realized it, but she had immersed herself so deeply in her time with Peter that night, that she hadn't thought of Tristan at all until she saw him standing off away from the crowd, watching her intently. She smiled at him, but it was a swift smile, and her attention was drawn back to the media who were asking her multitudes of questions.

Emmaline and Peter spent the better portion of the evening talking with other politicians, supporters, reporters, and guests. Their time seemed to go by so swiftly, and yet it seemed to slow down so much when they had brief moments alone together. Peter took every opportunity he could to touch her, to hold her hand, to wrap his arm around her, and whenever he thought he could fit it in appropriately, he kissed her cheek or her hand, and once more, after they had been talking to a news crew in the lobby, he kissed her mouth; softly, sweetly, just for a long precious moment, but he held onto each chance and made the most of it while he was able to. She kissed him back when he kissed her, and while he was certain that it was part of the show, her physical response to him made him feel as though there might be more feeling in her than he had first thought. The realization of that made his heart beat faster, and gave him the tiniest seed of hope, deep within his heart.

One of the reporters talked with them while others listened in and he brought up the issue concerning the current Governor's wife. "The Governor continues to bash you for your past indiscretion with his wife, stating that you have no morals and are not fit to lead the community. What do you have to say about that?"

Peter pulled Emmaline close to him and smiled. "I would say that we have all made mistakes in our pasts, and while I will always regret that one, it is not the sole defining trait of my character. I have moved on from that incident and I have found and married an incredible woman who loves this city and its people as much as I do, and together she and I will build this city back up to the heights of its glory again. The only thing I love more than New Orleans is this woman in my arms. She has changed me into a man who won't let this town down again."

The reporter grinned at him and Emmaline felt everything in her stop suddenly. Peter was able to turn a phrase quite easily, and he was excellent at speaking with the businessmen, politicians, and reporters that hovered around them hungrily, but he never lied. He had never spoken a word that he didn't mean, or that wasn't true. She had realized that right away. His comment about loving her more than the city caught her totally off guard. She tried not to show the surprise on her face, her smile only wavered slightly, but inside she was spinning in chaotic amazement. He wouldn't have said it if he didn't mean it, she thought to herself in wonder. She tucked it away into the back of her mind to consider later, and returned her attentions to the people before her, but when she looked up into his sparkling green eyes again during the rest of the night, it was there in her mind, and she wondered endlessly about it.

At the end of the night, Nelson asked Tristan to ride home with him, and Tristan grudgingly obliged.

Peter and Emmaline stayed until the last of their guests were gone, and then they went home together in the limousine, happily discussing the wildly successful evening. When they reached the house, he went into the drawing room for a drink and she went down the hall to her bedroom, but a few minutes later, her high heels discarded into her closet, she padded back down the hall to the drawing room to see Peter.

She walked in and saw him leaning against the back of the sofa. His shirt was unbuttoned most of the way and the cuffs of his sleeves were rolled up to his elbows. His hair was slightly tousled from him running his hands through it. He looked up at her in surprise and smiled warmly at her.

"You were so amazing tonight, Emma. Thank you," he said, waving to her to invite her in to join him. "I will never lose sight of the fact that none of this would even be happening if it wasn't for you. It's all because of you; every bit of it."

She laughed a little and walked toward him. He watched her body move under the snug green material that rippled and shined on her, and it made his stomach tighten.

"You made me feel as though I really mattered tonight," she said softly, reaching him and standing just before him.

He blinked in surprise. "You…" he said, "…you matter more than anything! More than everything else!"

Emmaline looked at him in surprise. "Do I?"

Peter stood up and stepped before her, lifting his hand and placing it underneath her chin. "I am nothing at all without you," he said softly. "I know that now."

Her breath caught and she didn't know if she could voice the question she had come to ask him. She didn't know if she really wanted to know the answer to it, because the answer might be more than she had considered. As she looked up at his face, she realized that she had to know.

"Peter," she said in a hushed tone, "earlier tonight you said something that I…" she took a deep breath and he waited for her to continue, "something that I was surprised to hear."

He knew what she would ask, and he felt himself coming to a crossroads. He didn't know how he could answer it without jeopardizing their arrangement.

"You said that you love me more than this city," she whispered, watching him closely. "Do you? Do you really love me?" She couldn't believe that she had spoken the words.

Peter looked at her, standing there in her emerald gown looking as beautiful as he could ever imagine, and he could not speak. He could not say what he wanted so much to say to her. He could not risk losing her, but he had to find a way to respond somehow. His eyes seemed to lock on hers and he could not turn away, and he could not ignore her question.

He stared at her for a moment, then smiled slightly and touched her cheek with his hand. "Who in the world couldn't love you?" Then his resolve crumbled and the nearness of her became an intoxication that he could not resist. Reason and rhyme vanished from his mind and emotion took over.

Emmaline felt the same heat she had felt earlier as he touched her, and she drew in her breath and lifted her hand to cover his hand as it touched her face. “But you…” she began to say, and couldn’t finish her thought, because he leaned toward her and pressed his lips to hers again. He could not hold himself back, nor did he want to. He had kissed her a few times that night, and not once did he kiss her as fully as he wished he could.

Her eyes closed as his lips touched hers and he pulled her into his embrace. She let herself become lost in the heat and strength of his body as his arms closed around her, and when he parted her lips with his, her heart began to pound. Peter‘s tongue met hers and everything in her felt like it was moving almost at the speed of light. His kiss deepened as their tongues entwined, and he pulled her body tightly up against his.

White hot flames grew in her belly and she felt drawn to him as though he might have been her center of gravity. His mouth stole her breath away, and her hands somehow found their way around him, holding him in return. His hands moved over her bare shoulders and across her bare back, and her skin felt as though it ignited with heat wherever he touched her. Her heart was racing, blood pounding in her, and her body began to feel a need for him in the hot depths of her.

Peter was lost in his own ocean of desire, in the daydreams he had had about her that were coming to life in his arms. His mouth moved from hers and traveled slowly down her throat, kissing and tasting her dark skin as he went, while his hand moved to her hip, squeezing the curve there, and pulling her against the solid, thick form of his hungry desire for her. As his erection pressed against her body, she let out a gasp of surprise and a moan of need, closing her eyes and losing herself completely to the feelings that were rushing all throughout her.

That was when reality came rushing back to Peter and everything around him came into focus. Emmaline there in his arms, her head tilted back, her eyes closed, his mouth on her neck and his hand on her hips, holding her to his body, his erection pressed against her, and he realized that this was the crossroads. He could continue. He could pull her dress off of her and lay her on the sofa, he could run his hands all over her gorgeous body, he could spread her legs and enter her, and make love to her for the rest of the night, but all of his playboy years had taught him that the sun always comes up in the morning, and when it did, it brought reality with it.

Everything would be changed between the two of them. Everything would be totally different, and while he was finally able to admit that he was in love with her, she was not in love with him, and he knew it. She could feel angry or hurt, perhaps used, and that would only be the beginning of the trouble he would see, because he'd been honest when he said that everything good in his life just then was happening because of her, because she was in his life, and all of it was hanging in the balance. All of it would be swept away if she left him, if she felt like he was using her or taking advantage of her situation. He knew he could not do what he wanted more than anything, though she was ready for him and he was very aware of it. He could not make love with her that night, and the only thing that he could do, was to stop everything at that moment, if he was to save the future for both of them. Ration and passion are never bedfellows, he thought to himself.

Peter let go of her slowly, reining his heart back in and raising his head as he looked down at her. He withdrew his hands from her and took a deep breath as she looked back at him in utter astonishment.

It felt as though a cool wind had wakened her from a dream, and she blinked up at him, trying to discern what was happening. He immediately grew worried that he'd messed it all up, that she would run away and leave him standing there heartbroken.

"I'm so sorry, Emmaline, I didn't mean to get carried away with you. You just looked so beautiful tonight, and I guess old habits die hard with me." He gave her the slightest of smiles and turned away from her, trying to catch his breath and slow his heart down.

She stared at him for a moment and then realized what had been happening. He had let his lust for women out with her, and she had fallen for it. She had succumbed to him, like so many women before her. She felt flashes of shame and foolishness envelope her, and before those emotions took her over, she remembered something else.

"That wasn't just you," she breathed heavily. "That was both of us together. We didn't do anything I didn't want to do."

Her words felt like a dragnet, pulling him back to her, but he could not let himself do what he wanted so desperately to do; to hold her and make love to her, and so he began to walk away from her but she grabbed his arm to stop him.

"What just happened? What was that?" she asked him anxiously, looking up into his eyes.

He shook his head, looking at her with a hint of sadness in his eyes. "I let myself go too far with you," he said, and then he turned and walked out of the room, leaving her to stare after him.

Peter went to his room and took a cold shower, hating himself for letting his desires get the better of him. He could not risk losing her, and she was already interested in Tristan. He had no right to kiss her like she was his to kiss; his to hold. He was consumed with regret and he promised himself that it would never happen again unless she wanted him.

Emmaline watched the door close and felt hot tears stinging her eyes. She closed them and tried to settle all the varying emotions in her heart and mind. He was a Don Juan, a Casanova, a playboy, lover of women, someone she should stay away from. She wondered if he was right, and if he had played her, like he had done with all of his other women, but then she thought of the emotion and desire that had come from so deep within her and she knew that it wasn't just him seducing her. She had kissed him back, she had wanted him, and that wasn't from nothing. That was not because he had tricked her or romanced her.

She could not figure out where her desire for him had come from. She had been so wrapped up in the idea of Tristan, of his sweet and charming manner with her, his beautiful looks and his thoughtful considerate ways. He was her ideal man, she was sure of it; he was everything she had been looking for and he didn't even know it. They just clicked and they were so good together, but then she wondered how she could have been so powerfully drawn to Peter, so desirous of him, when he wasn't the right man for her at all. He didn't fit any of the characteristics that she had in mind for a husband, and she despised the kind of man that he had been before she was with him.

Emmaline walked to the sofa and sat down on it, confused and frustrated with Peter, herself, and the situation. She turned the whole situation over and over in her mind, looking at both men, thinking about them both and what they were to her, and what she wanted from them. She was so exhausted from the day that she fell asleep there on the sofa in a matter of minutes. Her dreams were mixed between the men and her, and she felt lost, trying to find her place.

Peter wrapped himself in a bathrobe and ran a comb through his hair. He walked out of his bathroom and decided to have one more drink before bed. It had been a long day and his heart was torn in chaos. He walked barefoot into the drawing room and began to pour himself a drink when he heard a soft noise and turned toward the sofa. From behind it, he could see bare feet poking out over the edge of it and he walked around the furniture, looking down at Emmaline as she slept there on the cushions in her emerald green dress. A smile grew on his face and he shook his head. Peter bent over and picked her up carefully, cradling her in his strong arms, and walked down the hall into her room. As he walked, she stirred and nestled her face against his bare chest, where his robe was partly opened. Her breath was soft on his skin, and warm on his heart.

He laid her on her bed and looked at her, loving her even more as he watched her sleep. He knew he had to be careful, but he couldn't resist leaning down to kiss her mouth softly as she dreamed. Her lips moved for a moment, and she kissed him back lightly, and then she fell into deep sleep and did not move again. Peter sat there beside her for a long while, his hand in hers, watching her, loving her, wishing that he could have her, and then finally he let her hand go, stood up, and left her room, closing the door softly behind him.

In her dreams, Emmaline was with him and he was somehow without clothes on above the waist. In her dream, she touched her hand to him and they kissed, and in her dream, he made love with her, and then she found herself alone, and it was cold without him.

*

Emmaline awoke to a knock on the door. She opened her eyes and discovered that she was still in her dress. She called out, asking for a moment, then undressed and pulled a satin robe on and answered her door. Tristan was standing there with a large tray filled with food and coffee.

She smiled suddenly and laughed, and invited him in. They sat on her bed and she looked at the wide array of breakfast he had made for her again and shook her head. "I told you that you didn't have to do this! Thank you, though, it's really wonderful."

He leaned close to her and kissed her cheek. "I am glad to do things for you like this," he said with a smile. She began to eat and Tristan sipped his coffee.

"That was some party last night," he said quietly. "I think you both made quite a convincing couple to the public, as you always seem to do." He looked into the dark liquid in his cup and added, "You almost had me convinced as well."

Emmaline realized that he was a little hurt about how she and Peter were with each other at the party and she felt badly for him. "Tristan, we have to be like that with one another for the papers and the public. That's why he hired me."

Tristan nodded. "Well, it seems like sparks tend to fly brightly when you two are close together. I felt like I faded into the background quite a bit," he said, but then amended. "That's probably a good thing. It would be bad if anyone saw a connection between the two of us." He lifted her hand to his lips and kissed it.

She agreed, and enjoyed her meal with him, but she saw that there was a seed of jealousy in him that she hadn't known would be there, and it bothered her slightly. They were going to have to be careful with each other over the coming months so that their affections for each other weren't photographed by any press or seen by anyone who may destroy the charade that she was a part of. His jealousy was not going to help that at all.

"I need to work with Peter today, but when we are finished, I thought it might be nice to take you to dinner," he said, gazing at her with a smile.

Emmaline shook her head. "I can't go out to a restaurant and go to dinner with you unless Peter is there," she replied, somewhere between disappointment and frustration. "Shopping with you is one thing, but a dinner date is another thing altogether."

He grinned. "I'm one step ahead of you, lovely lady. Knowing that we can't be seen publicly, I arranged for a dinner picnic at a private property in the country where no one will be able to find us or see us, and where we can be together without interruption."

She wanted to go, she did, but she had made a promise to Peter. "Tristan, we agreed that we wouldn't see each other until after the results of Peter's campaign. We have to live up to that promise. We have to mean what we say." She stood up off of her bed and he followed her, reaching for her and pulling her into his arms.

"I know that, my dear, and I am holding back so much with you, but I don't think that the two of us having dinner alone together in the woods at a picnic is anything that would constitute breaking that word." His arms folded around her and tightened, and he leaned his head down and left soft kisses in a trail on her neck, and whispered in her ear, "It's just dinner, which we would eat together if we were here at the house. The only difference is that we would be eating it outside. No one will see us, and no one will ever know we were there." His mouth opened and his kisses moved from her neck to her shoulder as he carefully and slowly pushed her robe open further at the neck. She closed her eyes as the feel of his mouth on her skin sent the butterflies in her skittering around, and her breath began to shorten as her heart began to beat faster.

"We won't be seen by anyone." His lips were soft and his tongue was hot on her shoulder. "We won't be bothered by anyone." He slowly moved his mouth back to her neck, leaving wet kisses on her skin along the way. "We won't be heard by anyone." His kisses trailed up her neck to her mouth and he overtook her, kissing her deeply and hungrily as he held her snugly against him. His hands moved over her back, rubbing her muscles and massaging her as he kissed her. Her heart began to beat faster and she felt everything speeding up inside her, but it was completely different from what being in Peter's embrace had done to her. There was no white hot flame with Tristan, there was excitement, there were butterflies and nerves, but there was not the aching need that Peter had brought out in her.

Tristan moved his hand to her breast, cupping it partially and squeezing it softly. He ran his fingertips over her hardening nipple, moaning softly for her as he touched her. She felt like she was going to lose her breath completely. His hand moved to her hip and he squeezed her gently and then lifted his hands to her face and looked into her eyes. "You are so incredible, beautiful Emmaline. I could lose myself in you for eternity." He kissed her mouth once more and then spoke softly again. "Have dinner with me tonight, please." He touched his lips to hers and smiled. "*Please.*" He kissed her lightly again. "Please say yes." He leaned down and kissed her sensually again, holding her tightly, until she moaned softly and he slowly let his arms loosen. "Have dinner with me," he whispered, running his hands along her back and gazing at her with his intense blue eyes.

"Alright. We can have dinner together in the country," she said in resignation. He had kissed her into submission and she was embarrassed to admit it to herself. "But please make sure no one sees us."

"I promise that no one will see us," he said with a smile. "I have to go to work now. I'll see you later." He began to walk out of her room, taking the tray with him and then he smiled at her and winked. "If you want to wear that, I wouldn't be opposed to it at all." He nodded to her satin robe. It did nothing whatsoever to hide her piqued arousal for him. She giggled and pushed him out of her room, closing the door behind him.

Peter was going into his office and looked down the hall when he heard them, and he saw Tristan emerging from Emmaline's room with the breakfast tray and he saw her close the door wearing only her robe. His suspicions immediately took over and he was plagued by thoughts of them being together and making love. The idea ripped at him and he had to push it from his thoughts because he would be working with Tristan all throughout the day, and he could not try to work with the man while wondering if he had been touching and kissing Emmaline, and making love to her that morning in the very same bed that Peter had laid her down to sleep in. It was too much for him to allow into his mind. He worked as best he could with Tristan that day, but there was an air of tension between the two of them and it would not dissipate.

Emmaline answered the door partway through the day and discovered an enormous bouquet of roses for her from Peter. There was a card nestled into the flowers that read, "Thank you for making my life the best that it has ever been. I would never have reached this far without you." She smiled and wiped a tear from her eye, thinking back on his enormous success at the ball the night before. The crowds had welcomed him with open arms, and the people he talked to loved him and they loved his ideas. She set the flowers on the table in the foyer for everyone to enjoy, and she saw the day's newspaper there. On the cover was a photograph of the two of them together, waving at the crowds and the press from the podium, and beneath it were some images of them throughout the night. The first one in the row was an image of the kiss he had given her on the dance floor, the kiss that had set her on fire when they had danced together. The caption underneath it stated, "True love for this gubernatorial candidate!" She gazed at the picture and felt remnants of the heat that he had drawn up in her each time he kissed her. They looked like they were in love, and she could see for herself what it was that Tristan had been talking about. If she were the other woman, rather than Tristan being the other man, she would feel the same way that he did, were she to look upon her love interest with another person the way he saw her with Peter. She felt badly for him and decided that she would make a point of contributing to their evening picnic so that he felt her affection for him a bit more, to make up for him having to watch her in Peter's arms the night before.

Then she thought of being in Peter's arms in the drawing room when they got home, and how he had kissed her so passionately, how he had become a center of gravity for her, making her burn for him, making her lose her sense of self and feel as she had never felt with any other man before, and she had to catch her breath and steady herself with her hand on the table where his red roses arched out toward her. She reached out and touched her fingertip to their scarlet petals, breathing in their heady aroma. It was simple to see on the outside how he had sent them to her to thank her, but underneath the veneer of that, she wondered if there was a passionate and romantic undertone. Red roses; more than she could count, all arranged in a crystal vase for her. Was that friendship and thanks, or was it more? Was it a whisper of love and desire from him, or was it a misunderstanding on her part? He was, after all, one of the most notorious playboys in the whole city.

She remembered discovering him in the drawing room with two women, being intimate with both of them, not just one, and her stomach turned in disgust. It hadn't been that long ago, and it may have been an indication of his character, much more than the roses he had sent her today and the heated moments shared between them the night before.

Emmaline wanted to think on it more, and to try to discern what was really happening between herself and the two men. She had to be able to see past all the mystery and find the real love. Tristan was her ideal man, and she had been so sure that his love was what she wanted, but Peter made her want him with a burning desire that Tristan had not ever brought out in her.

When Tristan was through working with Peter for the day, he loaded his picnic up into his car and Emmaline joined him. He drove her out in the early afternoon sun until they wound around through trees and lakes and ended at a simple little cabin in the woods. It was a beautiful, peaceful place. She helped him unload what he had brought and together they walked into the cabin. It had one bedroom, one bathroom, a small kitchen and a deck that went around two sides of the house; one side was set over the water of the huge pond that the cabin was built beside, and the other deck stretched over the land. The trees in the wood were very old and had grown tall with long reaching branches that stretched out and canvassed much of the sky around them. The warm sunny afternoon was softer having come through the trees to reach them. There was a table for two set up on the deck facing the pond. Emma walked around the cabin and looked at all of it as Tristan began to unpack and then she went into the kitchen and helped him prepare their dinner.

"This is such a beautiful place," she said as she cut strawberries beside him while he made a salad for them.

"It is," he replied. "I wanted to take you somewhere where we could be alone and not worry about anyone catching us together or worry about any issues with Peter." He looked at her and smiled. "He is a good man. I don't want to disrespect him or his wishes in his own home. It's strange enough to want to be with his wife."

Emmaline shook her head. "Now you know that's just a business arrangement," she said, wondering if she actually believed the words she was speaking.

He sliced the sandwiches in half. "Is it?" Tristan asked. "You seem pretty content in his arms when the camera is on you both. In fact, it was such a convincing charade that I couldn't tell you were acting at all during the ball, but I guess that's why he hired you to be his public wife." He turned and looked at her with serious eyes. "I care a great deal about you, Emmaline, and I want to be with you, more than you would guess, but I have to know that you want me back that same way." He slid his hands around her waist and pulled her to him, looking down into her eyes.

"Do you want me that way?" He looked down at her hopefully.

The confusion in her swirled around again and she tried to hide it. "I think I do," she said in a soft voice with a smile at him. He gave her a wide smile and leaned down to kiss her while he cradled her in his arms.

"Good," he said, letting her go. "Let's talk about this some more after we eat." They carried their meal out to the deck and settled in to enjoy the late afternoon and early evening as they ate.

"This is such an unusual circumstance with you," Tristan said, his blue eyes looking out over the water around them. "I just didn't expect it at all. You were a big surprise. The first time I saw you in Peter's house, I was incredulous. He never has women there. I had no idea what relation you were to him, and it was fascinating to me that you were living there. I thought you were so brilliant that first day, helping us figure out a compromise for the way we were trying to merge the businesses. You just kept right on amazing me, and then when I found out you were going to marry him, it was like someone knocked the wind out of me. It really felt like a blow to the chest. I couldn't stand it, but I knew there was nothing I could do about it, but be there for you both as you tied the knot, and that's just what I did. When I saw you walk down that aisle, I wanted to reach out and stop you, pull you away and keep you for myself, but I couldn't, of course. I wasn't looking forward to staying at the house with you both for the project, but I thought that at least I could be around you some, and get to spend a little time with you, even if I couldn't have you, and bittersweet though that would be for me, I was willing to have even a little of you than none at all. Then, when I discovered that you were only in a business deal with him, that it wasn't a real marriage, I was stunned. It was like everything keeping us apart had vanished and you were there for me to have; like the timing was right, finally, and it was all going to work out. I felt like I had just been handed the most precious jewel in the world." He was watching her as she listened to him talk about how he felt about her. She was sitting there silently near him. He sipped his wine and covered her hand with his.

"It felt like everything was possible with you, especially after our day out shopping for your dress and our dance lessons in the garden, it just felt like you were there for me and dreams that I couldn't begin to allow myself were actually coming true." He waved his hand at the natural area around them. "This time, right now, here with you is another daydream coming true. I can hardly believe any of them are real, but they are, and you are here with me, and no matter if his ring is on your hand or not, your heart is here with me, and if that is all that I can have right now, then I'll take it, because I want all of you that I can have, no matter how much that is." He lifted her fingers to his lips and kissed them lightly.

Emmaline sighed and shook her head. "You are something else," she said with a smile. "I was wondering if you were ever going to come along. You seem like you are my perfect match; my other half of me, somehow, and it's so strange that you came into my life when you did, the way that you did, but if it hadn't worked out this way, we might never have met. Life is strange, isn't it?"

"It is indeed," he answered her. They cleaned up the remains of their meal and brought a bottle of wine out to the deck as they watched the sunset begin to color the sky with warm shades of orange, pink, and gold.

They sat together on the swing at the end of the porch in the peaceful evening and swayed back and forth on it, holding hands as she leaned her head on his shoulder. Together they sat in silence a while, just enjoying being together, and as the night began to descend upon them, he rose and walked with her into the cabin. They stood in the small living room and he pulled her into his arms and looked into her eyes.

"I want you to know something," he said softly. "I don't care how long it takes, I will wait for you to be free to be with me. I know he has his campaign and you have to be part of that, and part of his public image, and I know that it may take the whole three years of your contract with him, but I will wait no matter how long it is."

Emmaline felt her heart being tugged as she gazed up at him. "I don't feel like I could ask you to do that for me, it seems like such a big sacrifice. If you do wait, then I would be so happy about it, but if you find someone else in the meantime, don't let go of a chance for love because I'm tied up in this deal with Peter."

He lifted his hand to her face and caressed her cheek, looking deeply into her eyes. "I couldn't find love with anyone else, because I've already found it with you," he whispered. Tristan pressed his lips to hers and kissed her softly, the warm touch of his lips was tender and sweet. She closed her eyes and kissed him back, enjoying the closeness of him and savoring the pleasant moment in his arms. His fingers moved over the skin of her cheek and down the side of her neck to her collar, as his kiss deepened. The butterflies in her began to dance, as they always did when he touched her, and she wondered at the difference between his touch and Peter's.

Tristan slowly slid his fingertips from her neck downward into the narrow space between her breasts, touching her with a feather soft lightness. She gasped and drew in her breath as he began to open the buttons beneath his fingers. Emmaline felt a lightness in her as he moved his lips over her skin from her mouth down her throat to the high swell of her breasts. As his mouth and tongue moved over her flesh, the difference in feeling between his affections and Peter's grew like a chasm, widening more the further that Tristan went with Emmaline. His hands firm on her body, his mouth warm and hungry on her skin, and his arms around her felt good, but it was nothing at all compared to the flames of desire and need that Peter had created in her. It confused her, and she felt torn between the man who seemed so perfect for her, her ideal mate, and the man whom she was contracted to in marriage, but who did not want her or any other woman to tie him down in a relationship for the rest of his life.

Emmaline's thoughts went to Peter and she realized that she was developing feelings for a man who would not be satisfied with one woman; a man who did not want anything more from her than for her to pose as his wife. He didn't even want her in his bed, and yet she had begun to care about him in a way that she never had thought she would. She had begun to think of him in ways that made her breathless and warm, and she knew that she must never allow those feelings to grow. He was her employer, and that was all. He was her partner in a business scheme to improve his reputation, and that was all. He would never be a lover, and he would never fall in love with her alone, and for those reasons, she focused herself on Tristan at that moment, and knew that he should be the one to whom she committed her heart.

He lifted his face from the upper curve of her breast and looked at her with eyes heavy with desire. "Emma," he whispered with thick breath, "stay here with me tonight, please."

She considered it and wasn't sure what answer to give him, but she knew that she had to drive her heart toward him, and let Peter go from it altogether, and she thought that there must be no better way to do that than to make love with Tristan.

Emmaline lifted her lips to his and kissed him for a long moment. "Yes," she said, opening her eyes and looking up at him. He broke into a wide and relieved grin, almost laughing a little, and hugged her tightly to him.

"You are the most incredible woman! I have never wanted anyone the way that I want you." he kissed her in happiness, then scooping her up into his arms, he walked her into the bedroom and laid her on the bed, laying himself beside her.

Emmaline looked at him and curled her arms around his neck, leaning to kiss him. He kissed her in return and as they kissed, his fingers moved to the buttons he had not yet reached in the material over her chest. He opened them one by one, slowly and seductively, and as each one exposed more of her skin, he pulled the material aside and covered the revealed swell of her breasts with his tongue and lips.

She felt a bit shy and nervous as he pulled her bra away from her breasts and closed his mouth over her stiffening nipples. Tristan sucked at her, flicking his tongue over her and teasing her, until her eager nipples were rock hard and anxious for his mouth. He moaned in pleasure and moved himself above her, resting his body over hers as he kissed and sucked at her breasts. The moment he laid on her, she could feel his erection, stiff and beckoning as it pressed against her. He moved his hand from her full dark breast to the hem of her skirt and slid his fingers up her thigh as he kissed her mouth and sucked on her lips and tongue. The lightness she had felt began to turn like a kaleidoscope and she moaned softly as his fingertips reached the soft silkiness of her panties. He slipped his fingertips beneath the material and began to massage her slowly and gently as his mouth moved from her lips to her nipples and then drifted back again. His touch was warm and gentle and as he manipulated her body, she began to feel a dull ache that grew stronger as the pressure of his fingers increased and he slid them inside of her, making her moan and gasp. Her back arched as he began to move his fingers more swiftly and deftly within her, and as she lifted her body in pleasure, guided by the touch of his strong fingers, her breasts rose to his mouth and he nibbled and bit at her gently, making her cry out in orgasm, which made him more anxious for her, and he massaged his fingers around her and inside of her even more urgently until she clung to him and came again. The pleasure was exciting, but try as she might, she could not seem to get Peter out of her mind, and as Tristan pulled her panties off of her and moved himself in between her legs, pressing his clothed arousal against her body, she could not feel the rage of passion that she had experienced in her husband's arms, and it worried her that her feelings for Tristan might not be as strong as she thought they were.

He kissed her mouth hungrily, pushing and rubbing his erection against her in solid need, and as he did so, she knew that the feelings moving through her for him were not much more than lukewarm, and she stopped him.

"Tristan," she said in a quiet voice, "we need to wait for this. It doesn't feel right."

He raised himself up on his arms and looked at her face. “What is it? What’s wrong?” he asked. It was clear to her that he had no misgivings about making love with her and that the hesitation was fully on her side.

She felt so sorry stopping them in their endeavor to be together, but she knew it was the best thing to do. “I think I just need some time. It feels like this is happening too soon.”

He moved off of her and laid beside her. “Then we will wait. We have all the time in the world to wait and love each other when it is right for both of us.”

She buttoned her top back up and leaned over to kiss him. “Thank you,” she said and he kissed her back.

“I am glad to wait for you.” he said with a smile and touched her cheek. They rose up off of the bed and he drove her back to the house.

Emmaline didn’t see Peter that night, and later the next morning, she didn’t see Tristan until she was in the garden reading and he came to her and sat with her on the swing.

“Good morning, beautiful lady.” He hugged her close to him, kissing her lips softly.

“Hello, Tristan,” she said with a smile.

“I thought a lot last night about what happened between us, and I want to talk with you about something that you may not realize. I know I haven’t made it clear to you, and I want you to understand it fully.” He pulled her up off of the swing and wrapped his arms around her waist, holding her close and looking into her face.

Neither of them noticed that Peter had been walking toward them and when he heard them, he stepped behind a tall bush and watched them through it as they talked. His heart clenched when he saw Tristan holding Emmaline so close to him, but he said nothing.

"I love you, Emmaline, and as soon as I can, I want to marry you. The minute you are divorced from Peter, I want to make you my wife and spend the rest of our days together loving you with all of my heart." He dropped down to one knee and she stared at him, her eyes wide and her heart pounding.

Peter couldn't breathe or move. It felt like his whole world might just implode at any moment and there was nothing he could do to stop it. He had asked them to wait to date each other until after the results of the election so that he could have some time to figure out how to tell Emmaline that he loved her, but now it looked as though things had moved much further between the two of them than he had ever realized and it cut him to his core. He wished that he could reach through the bush and stop them both from making another move toward becoming a couple, but he knew he had no place doing it.

"Emma, please say that you will marry me and make me the happiest man in the world." He gazed up at her with hopeful longing and she wavered slightly as the shock of what he was doing and saying washed over her.

"Are you saying this because of what happened last night in bed?" she asked.

Peter closed his eyes in pain for a moment, and visions of her laying nude in Tristan's arms sliced through his mind and ripped at his heart. So they had already made love, he thought, and for the first time in his life, his heart knew what it felt like to break for love.

"No, I'm saying this because I want you to be my wife, and I want you to know that every day between now and whenever that happens will be one day too many for me. I would make you my wife right now if I could, Emma. I have never wanted anyone like I want you, and you need to know that. Please say you will marry me when you and Peter are divorced. Please promise you will be mine forever." Tristan kissed her hand and waited anxiously for her response.

She looked down at him and tried to find an answer. She tried to reason it out in her head and heart and all she could find was struggle. She pulled him to his feet and leaned up to kiss him, feeling like she could at least soften her answer to him with tenderness and love before she spoke.

Peter watched his wife and the woman he loved kissing his business partner and he knew that she was going to tell him yes. He knew that Tristan was what she wanted. She had even asked him if she could be with Tristan. He couldn't stand to be there any longer and watch her as she promised herself to another man. It would rip his heart right in half to hear her say those words to Tristan.

He turned and walked away quickly, heading toward the house as Emmaline stopped kissing Tristan. "I can't give you an answer today. I'm so sorry, but I need some time to think about what I'm going to do. I have to talk to Peter about it. I need to talk with my grandfather about it. This isn't as easy as I wish that it was, and you have said that you would wait for me. Is that still true? Could you please wait for me to give you an answer to that question after I talk with Peter and my grandfather?"

Tristan nodded and pulled her into his strong embrace. "Yes, my dear. I will give you all the time you need. If you would like me to talk with your grandfather as well, I will. I would like his permission to marry you." He kissed her sweetly, and then let her go with a smile.

He walked back to the house and she sat on the swing and lowered her face into her hands. She had no idea how she was going to come up with an answer for him, but she did know that the two men she needed to talk to would give her some good direction at least.

Peter watched her from his office window as she leaned back and moved the swing back and forth, her hand raised to her mouth in deep thought while she gazed into the distance. He was furious. His heartache had become a rush of anger at the turn of events. He was angry at himself for having been so stupid as to have needed to marry her in the first place, he was angry at Tristan for going after her once he had stolen her heart, he was angry with her for loving Tristan and wanting to be with him, and he was angry at them both for making love, but more than all of that, he was angry with himself for falling in love with her. He paced in his office, looking out of the window at her on the swing in the garden. He had a political career now because of her, and he didn't know if he could win without her, or if he did win, how he would manage running the governor's office alone without her support. He realized that she would be leaving and he hated to think of how empty the house would be without her, how he wouldn't be able to see her or talk to her, how she wouldn't be just down the hall any longer, or in the kitchen or garden. The house and his life would be so horribly empty without her.

He stopped his pacing and gazed at her. She was so serenely beautiful and she didn't even know it. He realized then that he had once truly believed that his life had been so full and so carefree, and that what he had thought was a happy and complete life was really a shell with no meaning in it whatsoever. It was when she had come into his world and changed it so tremendously that he suddenly had meaning to his existence. He had substance and happiness, he had desire and a fire for her and for life. It wasn't until he had her with him that he found true purpose to his existence, and now it was going to end, and he would be able to live as he had before if he wanted to. But he knew that he could never go back to that, that he could never live as he had, using women and playing with them like they were toys for his amusement. He could not go back to drinking and carousing and living without doing any real good. Even if she left and he won the election, he would still have the remnants of a life that he could devote to others.

He felt tears fall down his cheeks and his first ever heartbreak began to connect with his mind. Peter began to understand the true depth and meaning of love, and he knew that what he wanted more than anything, even more than Emmaline, was her happiness. If she wasn't happy and living a full rich life, then he could not be happy either, and it became clear to him that he would have to give her that happiness. He would have to let her marry the man she wanted so much, no matter how it broke his heart.

Peter realized, for the first time in his life, what true and real love actually was and it was overwhelming for him. He wept and pulled open the drawer of his desk, taking from it an eight by ten glossy photograph of him and Emmaline on the night of the ball. She was wearing her green dress, and they had just finished dancing. He had pulled her into his arms to kiss her, and the photographer had captured the incredible emotion of the moment they had shared and the passion in their kiss.

Emmaline opened the door of the office and poked her head in. She saw Peter sitting on the wide will of the massive window at the back of his office; the window that overlooked the grounds and garden. He was holding something in his hand and crying. She stepped in quietly and walked to him, but he didn't seem to notice her. She had never seen him show such vulnerability and deep emotion, and it touched her heart. She reached him and looked over his shoulder and saw that what he was holding was an image of him kissing her after their dance at the ball. The memory of it came rushing back to her in a heated wave and it warmed her just as he turned around to see her standing there.

He was startled and she saw a wide range of emotion cross his face as he looked at her, the most powerful of which seemed to be something like pain and desperation, but she couldn't tell what he might have been hurt by.

She reached for him, realizing that he must need some kind of comfort, and she wrapped her arms around his waist, laying her head on his chest. She breathed in his scent and it took her back to their night in the drawing room when they had kissed so passionately. She closed her eyes and breathed him in, losing herself in the heady scent of him and holding him tightly to her in her hug.

Peter was stunned by her sudden appearance and even more incredulous at her snug embrace around him. He wrapped his arms around her to hold her in return and as they encircled her, all of the emotion in him compounded immediately and came rushing to the surface. He was awash in grief, in love, in remorse, in need, in frustration and in desire. All that he could do was hold her as all of it overwhelmed him. He buried his face in her neck and hair, soothing himself with her closeness and the scent of her skin.

His breath on the side of her neck and the feel of his mouth so close to her was almost intoxicating to her and she closed her eyes as the heat she had felt in his embraces before returned and rose up quickly inside her. Her heart began to beat faster and her muscles tensed all over her body. She tried to take a deep breath to calm herself, but it only pressed her breasts more firmly against him and the feel of it heightened her state.

"What's wrong?" she breathed out against the curve of his ear. She could feel his heart pounding and his body tense up as well. He slowly lifted his head and looked down into her eyes; he was just inches away from her. His eyes wandered over all of her face, and came to rest on her full lips.

It was a moment he could not let go of or pass by. It was one of the most precious moments of his life, and he felt it. In a swift movement, he cradled her head in his hands and lowered his mouth to meet hers. She tasted sweet and her soft warmth was like a balm for him, easing every pain in his heart and building up flames of need in him. He kissed her as though it was his last kiss with her; he kissed her as though he had to share everything in him with her in that one brief touch and he gave her all the deep and powerful love he felt as his mouth moved desperately over hers. She moaned from deep in her chest as she kissed him back, and it ignited a need in him that he had never felt. He parted her lips with his and as he tasted her, he felt her grasp him more tightly and she returned his kiss with growing passion.

Emmaline had not expected him to kiss her at all, and when he had cupped her face in his hands and sealed her lips in his kiss, it had stolen her breath from her and fanned the flames of desire in her to the point that her body began to ache. She could not hold back the moan that escaped her, and when he heard it and felt it, it fueled the heat of his kiss and she felt vertigo take over inside her, and all she could do was hold on to him tighter.

Peter felt his erection as it grew thick and hard, and every time before, he had turned from her, he had hidden behind his desk or walked away from her, but this time he was locked in her arms, this time he was desperate because he knew it would be the last time that she was this close to him, and his desire was too intense. He knew she felt him against her when she gasped, but she didn't pull away from him in the least.

He groaned in need and his kiss deepened, but just as she responded to him, they heard voices outside the door and they broke apart and stared at each other, trying to catch their breath as the door opened and Nelson walked in with Tristan. Peter turned away from them and willed his body to relax so his desire wouldn't be obvious. Nelson and Tristan greeted Emmaline and she was slightly flushed and breathless, but she smiled at them both and then turned back to Peter just as he sat down at his desk.

"I'll come back and talk with you later. I need to go see my grandfather," she said as steadily as she could manage.

"Please give him my best," Peter said calmly, and waved as she nodded and walked out of the door.

Emmaline was in a hurricane of confusion and all she could think of was getting to her grandfather for some peace and direction. She drove to his house and all the while, aftershocks of heat and desire would make her tremble slightly as her mind and her heart returned again and again to the moments in Peter's arms. She had felt such fire with him, such need and hunger that it was almost overpowering to her. She couldn't imagine why he had kissed her; he didn't want her and he had already pushed her away once, saying that he didn't want to treat her the way he had treated other women, and that they needed to keep their relationship strictly business. The passion in his kiss spoke volumes to the contrary, and the feel of his body against hers as his desire grew apparent made her wonder what was really going on in him. There was no way it could be just business; not with passion like that.

She pulled up to her grandfather's house and went in to talk with him. He was happy to see her and they talked about how his health had been doing so much better and how he'd been out fishing and seeing his friends. He was happy and contented. After a while, he sat rocking in his chair and sipping his tea, then looked over the top of his glasses at her.

"What kind of bee do you have in your bonnet, young lady?" he asked quietly.

She sighed and looked at him with troubled eyes. "I can't hide anything from you, can I?" She smiled a little and leaned her head back on the chair she was in.

"I'm really confused about the situation I'm in with Peter and Tristan," she told him. "Tristan is the businessman who Mr. Turner leased his building to. He's Peter's business partner. Tristan and I have kind of been seeing each other and I really like him, and he really likes me. He wants to be with me, grandfather. He wants to marry me. I think I want to be with him, too, but now things are changing with Peter. He seems a little different with me, and I don't know what to do."

Henri nodded. "Yeah, I saw the papers that you were in for his party. I'd say things are changing between you two. It's one thing to sell your marriage to the public, but it looked to me like you were both buying your own story as well." He winked at her. "What is it that's confusing you?" he asked her, looking for the truth at the heart of it all.

"Well, I thought Tristan was my ideal man. I have a list of things… qualities and characteristics that I'd like to have in the man I wind up with, and I don't want to settle for anything less than that, and when I met Tristan and got to know him, I was sure he was the right man for me. I was sure that he had all of the characteristics I wanted in a husband, but then things began to change with Peter." She shifted in her seat and grew a little sad. "He was so bad, grandfather, you know that's why I had to marry him to help him with his reputation, because he ruined it. He has this need for women and I don't want to get caught up in that. I don't want to be with a man who wants more than one woman. I want a man who is dedicated to me and to us, like you were with Grandmother." She looked back at him and he nodded.

"When was the last time he was with any other women?" he asked.

She thought about it. "It's been a while," she answered him.

He nodded again. "How do you feel about him?"

Emmaline took a big breath and sighed. "He turns my head, grandfather. I had my sights all set on Tristan, and Peter just turned me right around. I can't barely keep him off my mind and out of my heart. He's lodged in there now and I just don't know what to do."

Henri rocked in his chair and took another long drink of his tea. "Well, Emma, you remember that story I used to tell you about the ugly duckling that became a swan?"

"Yes," she answered curiously.

"People are like that, Emma. Sometimes the ones that we think are ugly ducklings are really beautiful swans who are just waiting for the right person to see it in them. They don't always show it plainly on the outside like some others do. Remember when Peter helped me out here at the house when he brought that doctor in? That young man saved my life and he never talked to me about it and he never asked anyone anything, he just did it. He took care of things. He's a take charge kind of man. He has an ugly duckling past, and he had an ugly duckling reputation until he married you, but I'll tell you something, my girl, I would not be sitting here with you right now if it wasn't for him, and that's the truth."

Emmaline knew it, and she had tried to keep that fact out of her thoughts because it would sway her and she wanted to make an unbiased decision for herself.

"I'll say it like this, because no matter what I say, you need to make up your own mind. Sometimes we see things that we want, and other times we know there are things that we need. You have to figure out which one of those boys is what you need, rather than what you want, and you have to look under their outside feathers to figure out if you are looking at a swan or an ugly duckling. You focus on what really matters to you, and what you really need, and you'll make the right choice. You have good heart, baby girl, you need to trust in it."

She smiled and felt the peace and relief in his wise words comfort her. He was right. Peter had shown her sides of himself that hardly anyone had ever seen; good sides that were often overlooked because of his mistakes. The only downside to Peter was that he didn't want her back; or at least he said he didn't. His desperate kisses with her told her otherwise. She knew she needed to talk with him and then she could have a clearer idea of what she wanted to do.

Emmaline hugged her grandfather and kissed his cheek, and then left him and drove back to the house with a much lighter heart.

The Final Chapter

Tristan and Peter had been trying to go over their business plans, but there was a thick and awkward tension in the room that would not dissipate. Peter finally had to ask Nelson to give them some time alone, and when he left, Peter sat down at his desk and looked directly at Tristan.

"What's on your mind, Tristan?" he asked, feigning ignorance.

Tristan sighed loudly and pushed his hands into his pockets for a moment, walking over to Peter's desk and sitting in front of it. "You noticed," he said shortly.

"I would like to think that I know you fairly well, Tristan. Something is on your mind and it's something I have a feeling we need to talk about." He watched his business associate and waited for him to respond.

"It's Emmaline," he finally said with a big exhale.

"What about her?" Peter asked, waiting to see what Tristan was willing to tell him.

Tristan took a deep breath and looked right at Peter. "We have gotten close, Peter. I love her. I want to marry her."

Peter would have liked to think that he could have appreciated Tristan's honesty, and he knew the words were coming, but when they were air that had suddenly found a voice, they seemed to zing at him like poison tipped darts that blazed over the desk and hit him squarely in the chest. Peter did his best to keep his poker face on and not look as sick about it as he felt.

"Tristan, she's already married to me." He spoke as simply as he could in an effort to keep emotion out of it.

"I realize that," Tristan replied. "As your employee, though, Peter. I found out about your arrangement with her; it's a marriage of business and purpose, not a marriage of love. I want her because I love her, Peter."

Peter took a big breath and let it out slowly. He loved her too, but he wasn't about to tell Tristan that. "She's contracted to me for three years." He decided to keep playing it cool in an effort to dissuade Tristan from pressing him further.

"I'm aware of that," Tristan said quietly. "I want to ask you to let her go early. Give her a divorce so that she can be with me and have some happiness. You're going to wind up being the governor of the state; you will be busy with politics and you won't have time for a wife, especially one who isn't a real wife. Let her come to me, please Peter."

Peter turned his chair a little and crossed his legs. "How does she feel about you?" he asked, not wanting to know, but searching for a way out of the direction the conversation was going.

"She wants to be with me, Peter. She's only talking about staying with you because of the commitment she made to you. She's loyal," he added.

Peter looked sharply at Tristan. "At least someone is," he said coldly. "You are my business partner, Tristan, what made you think it would be acceptable for you to steal my wife away from me?"

Tristan's face grew anxious. "Peter, you don't love her! You have a bevy of women at your beck and call; you go out of town to be with other women and you have no connection to Emmaline other than your business relationship which just happens to be a marriage and even that is only a technicality!"

Peter didn't like the way that Tristan was speaking. "You want to watch your tone with me, Tristan. You know a good deal about me, but you don't know everything, and I am telling you right now, you are asking for too much. She is my wife, she is my employee, this is a crucial time in both my business and in my political career and I need her here with me. That's that. She has a responsibility to me and a duty, and you don't need to be filling her head with romantic dalliances. She's already committed, and as you just said, she is loyal, so let her be what she is and let her stay with what she has committed to, and don't try to sweep her away under your arm and leave me in the dust as the fool!"

Tristan narrowed his gaze at Peter. "You don't care about her at all! You are only interested in your project and your campaign! I love her, Peter! That should mean something, even to a cold hearted womanizing bastard like you! I want to marry her and love her for the rest of my life, and no matter what, that's what's going to happen! Don't make us wait three years because it might be better business for you! Where is your honor?"

"*My honor?* My honor! You are the one running around behind my back sleeping with my wife, seducing her right out from under me and trying to steal her away, and you want to know where *my* honor is? I have always thought of you as a good man, Tristan, but I can't overlook your underhanded actions while you have been a guest here in my own house," Peter shouted as he grew deeply incensed.

Tristan stood up and began to pace. "I am not sleeping with your wife! We haven't been intimate other than kissing! Peter, I feel strongly enough about this that I will draw this line right now. Either you give her a divorce and let her marry me, and we will continue our business, or I will walk out of here and our business partnership will go no further. It's your choice, Peter. I want her, and she will be my wife or we will be through from today forward." He planted his hands on Peter's desk and glared down at his friend and business partner. Peter had been enormously surprised and relieved to learn that they had not slept together, but it did not deter his course an inch.

Peter stood up and straightened his jacket, then looked coolly at Tristan. "If that's how you feel about it, then I suggest you begin to pack. She is not leaving this house, and she is not getting a divorce before the three years of our agreement are up. I am sorry to see that you have brought it to that level, but the choice is yours. Stay if you like, leave if you like, we can continue as business partners or end the days that we will work together, but I am telling you right now," he walked around the desk and stood nose to nose with Tristan, "she's not leaving and I am not going to give her a divorce for you."

Tristan looked angry and resolute as he gritted his teeth and then answered, "Well, that's that, then. We'll leave and you'll be served papers for her divorce. I'll go make arrangements to be gone by tomorrow." He turned and walked out of the office and Peter watched him go with a heavy heart. He was truly fond of Tristan, and he hadn't been in the dark about their intentions; he had known what was happening, and he had seen and heard it with his own eyes, but he refused to back down if there was even the slightest chance that she might want to stay. He had been so mesmerized by her kiss before they had been interrupted that he thought maybe she might want him after all, and that perhaps he had been mistaken, but he had heard the two of them in the garden, and he had seen them together, and he knew that what she really wanted, no matter how she kissed him back when he locked her in his arms, was Tristan.

He felt his heart sink low. He would have to give her the divorce that she wanted because he loved nothing in the world as much as her, now, and what he wanted more than anything was her happiness above all else. If a divorce and Tristan were what she wanted, then that was what he would give her, quietly, without fuss or fight, without hassle or issue, and she could leave with him when Tristan walked out the next day.

Peter had kissed her goodbye; kissed her soundly, and with all the love for her that he had. If that wasn't enough to keep her with him, and if she wanted to go, then he would not force her to stay with him. He was no monster; he was only a man in love and if she did not want to be with him, he would not keep her caged.

Emmaline was sitting in the drawing room with a cup of tea and a book when Tristan walked in and closed the door behind him. She saw right away that he looked flushed and she stood up to greet him.

"Are you alright? What happened? You look as though there is something wrong!" She worried over him.

He came to her and wrapped his arms around her. "I'm so sorry, Emma my love, but there has been a change here at the house and with the business. Peter and I have come to an impasse and I'm sorry to say it, but we will not be continuing our business relationship any further than today. I will be packing and leaving tomorrow for San Francisco. I want you to pack and come with me. I love you, Emma, and we will get married as soon as we are able to, but in the meantime, I want you to come with me. You can file for a divorce as soon as we get to San Francisco."

Emma was shocked. "What happened?" she asked with wide eyes.

He shook his head. "I tried to talk to him about us, and I explained how much we love each other and want to be together, and he wouldn't budge. He is insisting that you and I have to wait until the end of the three years so that you can finish your contract with him and then he will grant your divorce and you and I can be together."

Emma felt panic rising in her heart. "I'm contracted to him for three years, Tristan, I can't just break that. I committed myself to him. It's three million dollars and my word."

"I'll pay it. You don't have to worry about that. Just come away with me, just…" He pulled her to him suddenly and kissed her hard, and the kiss felt off to her, as though something had fractured somewhere along the line and the lightness that he used to bring out in her was faded and dull.

She pulled away from him and he looked at her in surprise. "Tristan, my grandfather lives here. Everyone I know lives here. I love New Orleans, I can't just suddenly jump and desert it, I can't just leave it all behind, and I don't want to leave. This is my home, my city; my whole life. I can't move to San Francisco on a whim!"

He sighed deeply and nodded, sinking into a chair near her. "I understand. Listen, what if we do this. What if I leave tomorrow and then come back for you? What if I give you some time to say your goodbyes and take a little more time to make it right before you leave? I'll do that." He stood back up and hugged her to him. "I'll just come back for you in a few weeks and that will give you some time to tie up all of your loose ends, and then you will come away with me and we'll file your divorce papers and get married." He kissed her hard again, his grasp on her was tight and his eyes were intense. "Then you'll be mine; my wife, and I will love you, always." He kissed her once more and she felt the coolness of it and pulled away.

"Tristan, I haven't accepted your proposal of marriage yet, and I just told you that I am not going to leave New Orleans. When I said that, I meant that I am not ever going to leave it. If you want to be with me, we need to be here, because I'm never going to leave." She looked at him earnestly and he bit his lip and nodded.

“I understand.” He turned from her and began to pace, pushing his hands down in his pockets and sighing. “We’ll work it out. All the same, I’m going to go tomorrow and I will come back for you in a few weeks, alright?”

She looked at him in consternation and nodded. “We’ll see,” she answered him. She had absolutely no intention of leaving and no matter how she said it to him, he just couldn’t seem to grasp that. Perhaps when he had had some time to let the dust and emotion settle a bit, he would understand that and maybe he would consider living in New Orleans, but as for herself, there would not be a day when she didn’t live in her beloved home city.

He stopped pacing and walked toward her, then he reached for her and wrapped her in his arms again. “I’ll come back here and we’ll talk about it. We’ll work it out and then we will be together forever, and everything will be right.” He kissed her cheek and then let her go, and he turned and walked out of the room, closing the door behind him as though that were the end of the matter and it had been settled.

Emmaline watched him go in utter disbelief. How had he gone from being her ideal to being a bit obsessive? She looked at the door and thought of what her grandfather had told her. She decided that she needed to go and talk with Peter and listen to what he had to say about all of it. She had committed herself to him, and he was paying her, so her first priority for advice and insight was her grandfather and her second priority was Peter.

She walked out of the drawing room and into the foyer toward Peter’s office when she saw Nelson walk out of the office door and close it behind him. He shook his head at her and motioned to the office on the other side of the door.

"He's on a call right now; he will be a minute, Emmaline." He smiled at her and said, "Sit with me a moment?"

She nodded and they sat together on the wide bench in the foyer.

Nelson turned and looked at her carefully and spoke to her in a quiet voice, "You know, Emma, I make it a point to stay out of everyone's business here, but somehow that always makes me the center of it, so I always know everything that's going on. I understand that you have a vested interest in both Tristan and Peter, and I'm not going to give you any advice because that's your choice to make, but there is something I think you ought to know before you make any permanent decisions. I think it will give you some insight that you may never know otherwise."

She looked at him in surprise and waited. "What is that?"

Nelson leaned toward her conspiratorially and said in a near whisper, "Since the day you found Peter in the drawing room with those two women, he has not been with any other women at all."

She gasped in shock and stared at Nelson. She could barely have been more surprised. "But he went out of town for just that reason all those times! How can that be? It's been ages since then!"

"Oh, he's tried, believe me. He has gone out of town a few times trying to find some way back to his old life, but you, my dear, have stolen his heart, and that's a feat I never thought I'd see done. He hasn't been able to be with any other women because he only has one woman on his mind and in his heart, and that is you. He thought that if he tried to take other women into his bed with him, he could push you out of his system, but all he did was make it worse on himself. I just wanted you to know, he loves you, Emmaline, and what you know about him isn't the complete truth. He doesn't always explain himself to everyone, and he didn't want you to feel threatened or obligated or guilty in any way, so he never told you that he wasn't able to be with other women. He never told you that he doesn't want them because he loves you." Nelson stood up and took Emmaline's hands in his, lifted them to his lips and kissed them very lightly. "Now then, I'm off to take care of some things for Peter. He has a lot of changes going on right now. Please don't mention our chat to anyone." He smiled at her and she nodded.

"If you want to go in, feel free," he said, indicating the office, and then he turned and walked away.

Emma stared after him in astonishment and felt warmth enter her heart and begin to seep throughout her whole body. She wondered in amazement at how she had not seen Peter loving her before. As she thought about it, she could look back over the weeks that had passed, even at the wedding when they spent their day together and when he kissed her at the altar; he had loved her even then and she hadn't known it, but she could see it now as clear as day, and the knowledge of it wrapped itself around her heart and stayed there.

It seemed that she had two men to talk to again that day, and she started with the one that would cause her the most sorrow first.

Emmaline walked down the hall and knocked on Tristan's door. "Tristan!" she called out to him.

He opened the door and smiled at her, inviting her into his room. His suitcase was on the bed and he was filling it with everything he had. His blue eyes were bright and determined. She didn't know how she was ever going to get through it, but she knew she had to.

"Tristan, we need to talk," she said gently. He stepped close to her and looked at her face as if he were trying to read beyond what she showed him at the surface.

"What is it my love? What's the matter?" he asked with concern.

She turned from him and began to walk around the room, nearer to the window and she stood close to the wall and looked out of the glass into the grounds beyond the house. He walked up beside her and watched her carefully.

She spoke in a soft and kind tone. "I need to tell you that things have changed, Tristan. I told you that I needed some time to think about everything; to think about us, to think about being with you, about making love with you, about marrying you, and now I've thought about it enough that I have answers for you. I know what I need and what I want."

He slid his arms around her from behind and leaned over her shoulder, kissing her neck. "That's so good to hear. You want me to make love to you here and now, don't you…" He kissed her neck again and moved his mouth up near her ear, whispering to her as his hand rose and cupped her breast and his fingers squeezed it firmly, "that's what I want too, baby."

She pushed his hand down away from her and turned to face him. "No, Tristan, that's not what I want at all." She saw confusion in his eyes and face. "I came to tell you that you don't need to come back here. I'm going to stay and I'm not going to divorce Peter. I'm going to finish out my three years with him because I want to be with him, Tristan."

Tristan blinked in surprise and sighed. "So you really aren't going to live anywhere else. Alright, we will get a house here. It's fine. You can move in with me as soon as your three years are up." He pulled her into his arms and smiled down at her. "We can see each other in secret like we did at the cabin. No one will know, and then at the end of your time with him, you will divorce him and we can finally be married." He leaned down to kiss her, but she turned away and stepped back out of his arms.

"Tristan, I want to be here in this house with him as his wife. I care about him. I love him." She said the words as kindly as she could, but she had to speak them to him nonetheless; he just couldn't grasp what she was saying to him otherwise, because he was so set on having her for himself.

He stared at her in disbelief and the expression on his face transformed from one of arousal to one of shock and denial. "What?" he asked almost in a whisper, his eyes searching her face for some clarification and meaning.

She felt horrible about telling him the truth, but it had to be said. "I love him, Tristan, and I want to be with him, no matter how that has to be. He's the right man for me and I didn't know it before, but I have realized that and I know it now. I'm so sorry if you feel like I led you on, and I am sorry if you are hurt, because I never intended for that to happen, but I want you to know how things are and I wanted to be the one to tell you." She reached for his hands but he took a step back from her and stared at her. "I care about you so much, but I can't be with you because if I was it would be a lie. I'd be lying to both of us and I just can't do that."

Tristan shook his head and then stepped forward and reached for her shoulders. "This can't be! You and I were just talking about this in the drawing room! You are going to come away with me; you're going to be my wife! I love you! Do you understand that? I love you!" He seemed to be pleading and arguing. His grip on her tightened and he pulled her to him, but Emmaline lifted his hands from her shoulders and walked away from him, going toward the door.

"I'm so very sorry, Tristan," she said, turning to look at him and crossing her arms in front of her. "I thought that you were my ideal mate; that you were the man I wanted to spend the rest of my life with, but I can see now that I was wrong. I know you're hurt and I never wanted to hurt you. I'm sorry I couldn't see it before, but Peter is right for me, and nothing will change that."

He looked furious and hurt. "I changed everything for you!" He raised his voice a little and glared at her with tears in his eyes. "I love you! You were going to be mine!"

She shook her head. “I can’t be yours, Tristan. I am married to Peter and that’s how it will stay.” Then she turned and walked out of the room and closed the door behind her.

*

She took a deep breath to steady her nerves and calm herself and then she went down the hall and walked into Peter’s office. He turned from the window overlooking the garden and pushed his hands down in his pockets with a sigh. His jacket was hanging on his chair, his shirt was unbuttoned halfway down his chest and his sleeves were rolled up just beneath his elbows. He looked to her as though he was going through a really hard time.

She walked in quietly and sat at one of the chairs before his desk. “Rough day?” she asked, slipping her toe into the water to test the temperature.

He nodded. “Yeah, it’s been a rough day. I have had a parting of the ways with Tristan. He has other goals in mind that don’t align with mine, so he will be going in another direction on his own. I think he plans on leaving tomorrow. I’m sorry about that; I know you care for him a great deal. I’m entirely responsible for it.”

Emma watched him and waited as he rounded the desk and stood at the corner of it, looking down toward her. “I have a lot of changes to make for the business because of his departure.” He looked at her with a sad and tired expression on his face.

"There are some changes that we need to make to, in light of the changes that he is making." He continued with a serious sadness about him.

"What are those?" she asked pensively.

He looked down at his shoes and then into her eyes. "I'm going to grant you a divorce so that you can be free to make your own choices about the life that you want to live. You've done more for me than anyone else ever has and I want to give you your freedom. I'm having Nelson draw up the paperwork tomorrow, so that all we will have to do is sign it, and then you can go." He turned away from her and walked to the window, looking out silently onto the garden again.

"I'm going to give you the three million; you have more than earned it. There's a good chance I'm going to be the next governor of this great state, and I owe every bit of that to you." He spoke in a soft tone and it touched her heart. "I want you to take the money and your freedom and go be happy, doing whatever you want to do with… with whomever you want to do it with." The sadness in his voice was profound and made her ache.

Emmaline sat there looking at him and realized that he was making the changes in their agreement so that she could be happy and go with Tristan. It was the most selfless, generous, heartfelt thing that anyone had ever done for her and it made her heart ache and her eyes tear up. She rose up out of the chair and walked toward him, looking at the back of a beautiful swan who had been masquerading as an ugly duckling. It was then that she knew just how deeply she had fallen in love with him in her time with him and she knew without a doubt that her grandfather had been completely right about them. Everything about Peter had changed, right under her nose, and it was all because of her. She felt a deep and strong love that, like a river, sprang up suddenly in her heart and began to run wild for him; like it had been blocked off and the barrier had broken. She was amazed that she had not seen the obvious changes in him, but she was so glad she had discovered them before it was too late. She was so relieved that she had chosen not to be with Tristan.

"Peter, you don't have to give me the money or the divorce," she said quietly.

She reached up and touched his back and he looked down at his feet for a long moment and then looked back out the window, away from her. "I do, Emma, I have talked with Tristan, and I know how you both feel about each other. You love him and you want to be with him as his wife, so I do have to give you the divorce, and I want to give you the money. Like I said, you have most certainly earned it. Also, I have to apologize for what happened earlier. I'm so sorry that I kissed you again. I know we ruled out things like that and I had no business pushing myself on you the way I did. Please forgive me for that and know that I am sorry for it."

Emmaline kept her hand on his shoulder and looked up at the back of his head and spoke with a kind strong voice. "I'm not," she said.

He was still for a moment and then turned slowly to look at her. "What was that?" he asked in complete astonishment.

She lifted her chin and looked at him. "I am not sorry you kissed me. It was one of the best kisses of my life. I'm so glad you did it, because I love you, Peter, and I hope you kiss me like that again all the time. I'm not going with Tristan when he leaves and if he comes back it will be in vain. I'm your wife, and I want to stay here with you, because I love you."

Peter could have been knocked over with a feather, he was in so much shock. "Can this be real?" he wondered out loud. She just grinned at him and took his hands into hers.

"Emma," he whispered her name and looked down into her face, "I love you, too. I never knew it could feel like this, and I have tried to get you out of my mind and out of my heart, but the more I try, the deeper you get into me. I need you, Emma. I need you like the air that I breathe, but I was ready to let you go to him and leave me, because I thought you needed him. I thought he would make you happy. There is nothing I want more than your happiness." A tear rolled down his cheek and he wiped it away quickly, but he was never happier than he was at that moment looking at her as she stood there telling him she loved him.

Emmaline lifted her face to his and, laying her hands on his chest, kissed Peter's mouth for a long moment, and then stepped back to look at him. He stared at her for a long minute in utter surprise and then leaned over and swept her off of her feet and into his strong arms. She laughed joyfully and he turned his face to hers and kissed her in shock and complete happiness, and then he walked out of his office and carried her down the long hall to his bedroom, where he closed the door behind him with his foot and laid her on the bed. She looked up at him with excitement and rapture. She couldn't believe it was happening, but it was, and her heart flooded beyond overflowing with all the joy in her.

He leaned over her and looked deeply into her eyes. "Are you sure you want me rather than Tristan? I thought you were going to marry him." He had to ask her, to be sure.

She had never been surer of anything in her life. Emmaline lifted her hands up to his face and pulled it down to hers, pressing her lips to his smile and saying huskily, "I can't marry him. I'm already married to the man I love."

Peter laughed lightly in amazement and then moved himself next to her on the huge bed. He gazed at her for a long minute, hardly daring to believe that they were laying there together, and then he leaned over and touched his lips to hers, kissing her deeply, and the fires that he had brought up in her ignited immediately as she realized that he really was going to make love with her then. He touched her face and her neck carefully and gently, tracing her features, caressing her skin and hair, and somehow he managed to hold himself back as he peeled her clothes off of her a piece at a time, as though he was unwrapping a precious and priceless gift. For the very first time in his life, Peter began to experience the wonder of making love rather than just having recreational sex with a meaningless partner or two. It was life changing for him.

As he took the last pieces of material from her body, he stared at her in awe, his hand gently brushing what he had wished for and desired for so long. “I imagined you so many times,” he admitted to her as she smiled at him, “but never in my best dreams did you look this beautiful.” He touched her lips softly with his and ran his hands over her skin as he felt all of her in his reach. “I love you,” he said as he kissed her and then he began to canvass her body with his mouth. He moved from her luscious and full lips down her throat to the generous swells of her breasts, tasting her nipples and sucking gently on them as she raked her fingernails through his sandy blonde hair. His hands squeezed and massaged her breasts, cradling them close to his face until he moved himself down to the valley beneath her belly.

Peter slid his hands over her thighs and moved them apart, running his tongue over the inner areas of her legs and making her gasp with need and delight. He kissed her body and painted his wide hot tongue over the core of her until she called out his name, coming passionately as his hands clung to her hips and legs and his tongue was fervently exploring her inner depths. She had never experienced pleasures such as he was giving to her and before he could enter her, she laid him down and swallowed the thick and solid length of him, sucking on him and teasing him, drawing him to the brink of joy and then relenting enough that he was desperate for more of her and rolled her over onto her back underneath him.

He rose above her and rubbed himself along the outside of her, feeling the moistness of her body as it ached and longed for him, and then he slowly entered her, pushing himself into her inch by inch and making her writhe in his arms with desire until she was filled with him, and they both closed their eyes and soft sighs of pleasured bliss escaped them. He moved with a rhythm of love inside of her and as he pushed himself deeply into her body, she wrapped her arms around his neck and hugged him tightly to her. Together they swayed and rocked and she could not count the times that she clung to him in ecstasy, as orgasm after orgasm shuddered through her time and again. Her hands moved over his light skinned, toned and muscular body, vacillating between sweet caresses and hungered need. She made him clench to her tightly when the feelings were too intense, but he would not let himself reach that pinnacle of love because he wanted to remain in her body for as long as he could, feeling her underneath him, above him, around him, and burying himself in the depths of her fiery heat. His hands and his mouth explored every part of her as the two lovers learned one another and loved each other until he could not hold himself back. Finally, he let go of a powerful release into her body, holding her tightly to him and losing the very last of his old life at the same moment that he was given the gift of a new life, a life with the woman of his dreams, his wife.

He discovered a love and passion that he did not know existed, and he learned that the more he let go of himself in her arms, the more he found himself, and the more he realized that there would never be another woman that could make him want her like Emmaline did. He was almost dumbstruck by her beautiful heart and her breathtaking body, and somehow, no matter how much of her flesh he licked and tasted and touched, he continued to want more of her. It was an insatiable hunger between them both that was never appeased.

Mere minutes after he had collapsed in bliss with her in the bed, he was aroused again and she was stunned. "So soon?"

He grinned at her. "I've wanted you for so long, and I just can't get enough of you. I'm never going to have enough of you." Before they could say anything else, he was inside of her again, and their white hot flames of desire were blazing in and around them as they held each other and wrestled in their lovers tangle.

Emmaline knew that she had chosen the right man and she marveled at the lesson she had learned about seeing people for who they really are rather than who they might be perceived to be. "We better tell Nelson not to work on the divorce papers, then," she said with a wide smile, and he laughed and kissed her.

"No. We have to stop the divorce right away." He pulled her into his arms. "I'm never going to let you go." He kissed her again and held her close to him.

They finally fell asleep together and slept cuddled in each other's arms, and when dawn broke, they made love again with happy sighs and blissful joy.

Tristan had already gone when they finally emerged from Peter's bed the next day, and Emmaline silently wished him well and hoped that he would be alright and find some happiness without her.

He sent her a message many weeks later, telling her that he was heartbroken, but he wanted her to be happy and if Peter was what she wanted, then it was Peter that she would have, and they did not speak again. There was never a time in all the years to come in her life with Peter that she ever regretted the choice she had made or second guessed what might have happened had she gone with Tristan.

Their marriage became more real every day as they learned to live together and thrive as one. They worked on the campaign with eager and determined hearts and hands, and when the election finally came, she was at his side and under his arm when he discovered that he had won the election in a landslide. It was an ironic turn of events when the old governor had to shake Peter's hand and welcome him to the new office.

It felt to Peter as though he had finally come full circle and he could see, far after the fact, that each of the events that had happened had led up to where he had found himself, and, as Governor for the next few years, he always went on record to say that without Emmaline, he would not be nearly the man he was – and he would never change a moment of it.

THE END

Hey beautiful!

I really hope you enjoyed my novel and I would really love if you could give me a rating on the store!

Thanks in advance and check the next page for details of my other releases. :)

CJ x x

ALSO BY CJ HOWARD

THE BILLIONAIRE'S LOVE CHILD

On the surface, Billionaire Kevin has it all. He is rich beyond his wildest dreams and has the perfect trophy wife to go with it.

However, there is one thing he wants more then anything else in the world... A Child.

Only problem is, his wife refuses to give him any children and does not have any plans to do so ever. A divorce would be too messy for a man of his wealth so Kevin has no choice but to take drastic action.

He hires a surrogate with a **TWIST.**

He will father a baby with her but in this arrangement she will get to keep it. In return, mother and child will be supported financially for the rest of their lives. They will never need or want for anything, just as long as Kevin can fulfill his dream of being a dad.

For the beautiful and curvy Marina this is the ideal arrangement for her. She has always dreamed of being a mother but has never met a man worthy.

Kevin and Marina are about to embark on a very unique arrangement. One that promises to blur the line between love and convenience. Can such an arrangement exist without feelings getting involved? And can Kevin really stand by and watch his love child grow up without being involved directly?

Printed in the USA
CPSIA information can be obtained
at www.ICGtesting.com
LVHW010857280124
770147LV00009B/811